Copyright © 2009
A.C. Boyan
Front and back cover designs
And photographs by A.C. Boyan

ISNB 0-9671795-2-1

CODE NAKED

A. C. Boyan

Chapter 1

The Reunion

A State Department employee in Washington D. C. sat at his kitchen table. He had just finished breakfast on a Saturday morning and his thoughts were about how he would take advantage of a sunny spring day, when the phone interrupted him.

"Yes."

"Is this the Jim Grant that worked for the U. S. Embassy in London?"

"Who am I talking to?" Could it be possible?

"Do you remember a girl named Greta?"

The name Greta released a flood of emotion that left him standing in a vacuum.

"Of course, it's been so long, how did you find me? My name is Jack Dunn now."

"Yes, and mine is Tanya. I wasn't able to leave Russia for a long time. Now I can, and with friends in the right places I found you. I'd love to see you and talk to you, is it possible?"

"Yes, where?" Jack wrote down the address.

Fifteen years ago they met in London, he was an employee at the U. S. Embassy and she, an exotic dark haired beauty, worked for the Russian Embassy. He was smitten the first time he saw her at an Embassy function. Mutually attracted they began dating. It was hard to distinguish their relationship as personal or professional because each was a spy. She was KBG and he CIA.

They had abruptly parted without explanation. She was recalled to Russia and he to the U. S. His cover had been exposed after he killed a KGB agent, preventing the agent's assassination attempt. Two KGB agents attempted the assassination and one got away with a good look at him.

A forty two year old widower, with graying black hair and a square, weathered face, renewed memories that were dormant for so many years. A long lost love rekindled after all these years. He trembled as he drove down Wisconsin Avenue. His emotions intensified when he heard the next song on the radio. 'The First Time Ever I Saw Your Face–' My GOD, did she feel the same way?

He would know in a few minutes. He left his car in the underground garage at the Bellevue Hotel, took the elevator to the twelfth floor and knocked on room 1240.

She stood in the doorway and said, "Jack?"

"Tanya." He fought the urge to hug her. He wanted to be sure she felt the same.

"Oh, Jack." When she lifted her arms, he made his move. They stood hugging, tears misted his eyes. In an instant fifteen years vanished. He was in a time machine. She was the beauty he fell in love with.

She took his hand and led him into a suite with a spacious living area. An L shaped couch and coffee table faced a fireplace. A desk and chair occupied a corner and on the outside wall a large window framed a beautiful view of the city.

"Sit down Jack," she pointed to the couch, "can I get you a drink?"

"Thanks, maybe that will calm me down."

"Jim nervous, I mean Jack, man of steel, I'll be right back."

Jack got up and went over to the window. As he admired the view he sensed Tanya's presence. When he turned around, there she stood. Her beautiful face transformed to the ugliness of hate. In her hand was an automatic pistol.

"Not so professional, huh, Jack. Talking to the victim before you kill him, but I want you to know why, Jack, revenge. You killed my husband, the only man I ever loved."

"Leonid, the assassin?"

"Yes Leonid. My beloved Leonid."

Two loud thumps came from the door. A voice called out, "Maid service, maid service."

It distracted Tanya and in that instance Jack's training instinct took over. He leapt at her and grabbed her wrist in a twisting action. They both fell over the coffee table and landed hard. Tanya hit him with her left hand and then rolled from under him, in doing so the gun went off hitting her. The struggle was over, her body lifeless.

Jack got up and stood looking down at her. His question was answered.

No, she didn't feel the same way.

Chapter 2

Incident Report

Outside in the hallway the maid stood frozen in astonishment, Jack nodded toward the room and said, "Call 911, there's been an accident. When he reached his car he got in and pulled out his cell phone. He called a number that was given to him when he left the CIA and took a job with a new identity as a government employee. It was too be used for emergency situations.

"Jack Dunn, Jim Grant 3714, code naked."

The phone went silent except for keyboard clicks that could be heard in the background.

"Incident?" the man said.

"Fatal shooting an hour ago, Bellevue Hotel Room 1240."

"Victim?"

"Greta. Now Tanya. She was a KBG agent I worked fifteen years ago in London."

"We'll send a contact over to work with the Metro Police. Meet me tomorrow morning at ten, Bethesda Barnes and Noble. I'll be sitting next to the fountain."

"Recognition?"

"I'll be reading the *Da Vince Code*, nothing like a good thriller. Ask me if I've read *Angels and Demons*."

Chapter 3

The Big Picture

It was a busy Sunday morning at Barnes and Noble. The bookstore faced a corner and had a large flagstone patio in front of the entrance. A stone fountain served as a focal point around which people sat in chairs, or on the circular, low stonewall enclosing the fountain. Jack walked directly through the large glass doors and turned left. He stopped at a book case advertising the last chance to buy these books. He picked one up, placed it in front of his face, and scanned the patio area. Even if the man wasn't reading the *Da Vinci Code,* Jack would have picked him out. Short graying hair, taut face, sunglasses, and wiry build. As he went out the entrance he thought, it takes one to know one.

He sat next to the man on the wall, angled his body and splashed his hand in the water. "Ever read *Angels and Demons*?"

"Yeah, but I like this one better. Let's go inside and get a coffee."

After buying two coffees, Danish and a brownie, they sat in the far corner of the café. The CIA man spoke first, "By the way, I'm Bill Thompson."

"Glad to meet you. How long have you been in?"

"Ten years."

"What happened to you? I read you left shortly after you came back."

"It got to be too much for my wife. We wanted to start a family. That's a tough career for a family man."

"Did you?" Bill asked.

"No, that never materialized." Jack watched Bill as he eat, drank, and moved his eyes to catch everything going on around him. Definitely a man who had worked in the field.

"I've read the file on the London incident, but my question is why didn't you call us when she contacted you?" Bill said.

"What the file doesn't show is the fact that we were romantically involved. I didn't know until yesterday that Leonid was her husband. After all these years I just thought it was a lover's reunion." Jack sighed and reached for his coffee.

A student pulled two tables together next to theirs and put his computer down. Three more followed with their drinks and books. Bill made eye contact with Jack and nodded a signal to go. Jack followed him to the refill station and then to a group of empty tables at the opposite side of the café. "So what happened in the room?" Bill asked.

"She pulled a gun and said she was going to kill me for killing her husband. We struggled and the gun went off."

"That was not her primary reason for being in the District. Her being here on other business gave her the opportunity to get to you." Bill drew closer and rested his elbows on the table with his hands around his coffee cup.

"How do you know that?" Jack asked.

"We checked out the information we found in Tanya's purse at the Bellevue which led us to her room at the Fairmont. Tanya Slutskaya and Gregorie Yaroker are representatives of a Russian boat manufacturing company. Tanya and Gregorie have been suspected of dealing in black market Russian weapons for years. That alone is not too significant, but the fact that terrorists' communication intercepts concerning a strike in the D.C. area has increased and their being here is very significant. We've check out Gregorie and his trail ends in London after the assassination attempt you prevented. Gregorie could be Vladimir the assassin who got away."

"Vladimir?" Jack's body stiffened and his eyebrows lifted. "If Gregorie is Vladimir, the combination of Vladimir and Tanya, widow of Leonid, presents a whole different perspective. Vladimir is the only professional assassin I know of that worked with a partner. That's how he escaped capture when I took out Leonid. He plans his hits in such a way that the partner is always in the forefront of the action when the plan goes down."

"A shield," Bill said.

"More a decoy that's expendable. No, I don't think black marketing is their game here. Especially if Gregorie is Vladimir and he teamed up with Tanya. Once an assassin, always an assassin. There would be a lot more money involved. If that's what his objective is now, he's going to have to go it alone. He won't like that."

Bill smiled and said. "Sounds like Company thinking."

"Maybe my thinking but not my body and nerves. Was Gregorie staying at the Fairmont?"

"No." Bill's face showed disappointment. "He must be booked at a separate hotel. The Bellevue hotel was booked under another name."

"That's Gregorie's MO. He always has a safe house during his operations. Tanya was going to make good use of it."

"That's where you could help, you know how he operates and you have seen him a number of times."

"Isn't that a problem for you investigating on domestic soil?" Jack asked.

"No. The subjects are foreign and it has terrorist implications, plus, we're working with the FBI."

"Well I couldn't possibly be any help to you." He thought about what happened yesterday, the adrenalin rush and how his body came alive when forced into a survival mode. It had been years since all his senses reached that extreme level of intensity. Back then a daily possibility, back then he was much younger.

"On the contrary, you developed excellent information on Leonid and Vladimir. You tracked them down and prevented an assassination. Another thing to consider is the fact Vladimir, who now may be Gregorie, is a cold-blooded killer. He knows you can identify him. Plus the fact, if they are working with the terrorists, your exposing and killing Tanya may have jeopardized their plans. He may be a little upset with you right now and has killed for less reason."

"No thanks. I've got a good job where I don't have to keep looking over my shoulder. I'll leave that type of work to the professionals."

"What do you do for the State Department?"

Jack knew Bill had the answer, just as Bill knew to schedule their meeting three blocks from his apartment in Bethesda, and Jack had used this technique in the past to keep someone talking.

"Intelligence and research. Very interesting work and I just couldn't up and leave it." Jack said.

"I'm sure the Company and the State Department could work something out. It would be a special services contract. A temporary assignment."

"Yesterday was more emotion and excitement then I've experienced in a long time. It will take me awhile to get over that."

"You want to talk to someone about it?" Bill said in a sincere tone.

"No, I'll be all right."

"Call me if something comes up."

“Right.” That 'something' gave Jack a sinking feeling.

Chapter 4

Where's Tanya

A small nondescript man wearing a polo shirt with a sport coat walked into the Fairmont Hotel about noon on Saturday. He took the elevator to the ninth floor, got out, turned right and took the stairwell back down to the eighth floor. He checked the room-numbering guide on the wall and headed in the direction of room 825. When he arrived at the room, a man stood at the door with a small bag in his hand. Another man opened the door and the man with the bag went in.

He went back to the stairwell and walked down to the seventh floor and took the elevator to the lobby. He walked over to the bell desk and said he was there to pick up Tanya Slutskaya but she was not in her room. He asked the bellman if he had seen her leave. The bellman said she left earlier in the morning. He called a cab for her. Gregorie took some bills from his pocket and asked if he knew where she went. The bellman smiled and said, "The Bellevue."

It didn't take long at the Bellevue posing as a news reporter to bribe a maid into telling him a shooting occurred in room 1240.

Gregorie put the pieces together. Tanya had told him about the plan to kill Jack. Gregorie had worked with Leonid on quite a few contracts, which was unusual for that occupation, and Leonid had become a trusted associate. He had no problem with her plan and actually welcomed the idea, but it was to be done after their present contract was executed.

Tanya jumped the gun. Now he had to go it alone and Jack, the man who killed two of his trusted associates, was a problem that would have to be dealt with.

Chapter 5

Monday's Always a Downer

Monday is always a downer for working people, but this one for Jack carried with it a dream like quality of his weekend experience. Did that really happen? As he sat at his desk and looked around his office, he realized how he took for granted the comfort and safety of his work environment. He liked Bill and respected him and all the others that worked in that clandestine world doing tough work protecting our lifestyle. It was against his nature to turn Bill down.

After work, he stopped at the ticket vending machine in the subway and recharged his Metro ticket. His Audi RSX was in the apartment garage most of the time and the Metro Red Line took him from his apartment in Bethesda to work and other events going on in Washington.

On the Metro, he sat down and placed his gym bag between his legs. Three nights a week he got off one stop from his apartment to go to the gym. The other nights and the weekend he got his exercise from jogging or riding on the bike trails in the park.

The walk from the gym to his apartment was a mile and he used it as a cool down period. It passed by a string of ethnic restaurants and on many nights he would dine at one of them before he went home, but tonight one of his favorite TV shows was on and he didn't want to miss it.

With his gym bag in one hand and his security card in the other he stood ready to unlock the gate. "What the hell you doin', you crazy man?" Jack turned; the voice came from a homeless man on the ground in the bushes with another man standing over him with a gun. The gun was pointed at Jack. Instinctively he dropped his gym bag and reached for a gun he hadn't carried for fifteen years. The man on the ground got up, bumped into the man and deflected the shot he made at Jack. Then the man turned on the homeless man and fired two shots into him. When the man turned back—Jack was gone.

Chapter 6

Second Incident

　　"Jack here." He called Bill the second time in three days.

"What's up?"

"Another incident." Jack described the incident. "What's my cover?"

"At the entrance you heard two homeless men arguing and then gunshots, you took off–only if asked. Did anybody see you?"

"I don't think so. I went right back, retrieved my gym bag and went to the apartment. I don't know if the body has been discovered yet." Jack walked over to his window that looked down on the entrance to the building. "I don't see any official vehicles on the street. The body's not visible either. There are a lot of bushes and trees along the front wall."

"Stay put tonight. I'll meet you tomorrow at seven in the diner next to the Metro station."

Chapter 7

A Change of Heart

Bill signaled him from a corner booth. No sooner had Jack sat down than the waitress asked. "Ready to order?"

When the waitress glided away with their orders Bill asked. "Did you recognize him?"

"No. Not enough light. The trees and bushes block the entrance lights."

"What do you think happened?"

The waitress brought their coffees and they both took a drink.

"I think he was waiting in ambush and when I came he made his move and stepped on the homeless man. It's not uncommon to see one sleeping out there." Jack continued in a somber tone. "A homeless man saved my life."

"Do you think it was Gregorie?"

"No doubt."

"This simple out in the open attack doesn't fit the pattern of a methodical assassinator." Bill started on the breakfast the waitress placed in front of him.

"No, but Gregorie, yes. He doesn't over think. He will use a simple walk up and shoot technique. Sometimes the simplest and most direct method is the best and in Gregorie's case, he reduces the complex to the simple."

"As simple as this attack seems, he did have to find out where you live and your schedule on Mondays." Bill's face tightened. "I think we'll keep a watch on you. Any problem with that?"

"No."

"Any other way we can help?"

"I think I'm going to help you find Gregorie and that will be self-serving."

"Then you're aboard?" Bill's pale blue eyes brightened.

"I am and the first thing I'm going to need is a weapon."

"What's your preference?"

"I'm from the old school, a Walther PPK. It's concealable, accurate and I've trained with it. I wish I had it last night."

"Stop by the office after work." Bill took a card from his wallet and slid it across the table.

Jack picked up the card and read it. The American Association of Cacti Growers (AACG). He broke out in a smile and chuckled.

Chapter 8

Where do I Begin

When he arrived at work, he went directly to the small conference room where his staff waited to give their morning progress reports. Their work consisted of gathering intelligence and doing research prior to diplomatic visits and policymaking. The department was organized into units with each unit made up of employees who utilized their special skills in Internet activity, wireless communication, broadcast monitoring and statistics. The information requests came from the White House, senators, and diplomats.

Todd Hunter, a genius with the computer, gave the first report. He had hair with a life of its own and a tall lanky build. Jack had a lot of respect for his abilities, and always thought he would look more natural on a skateboard than in the State Department. His report concerned a new organization protesting outside the American Embassy in London called 'Hands Together for Global Peace'. The information he uncovered showed it was funded and organized by an anti American group working out of Palestine called 'Infidel Blood Bath'.

Jack was pleased with this group of employees. They were young, intelligent, creative, team players that followed a project to its end with tenacity. At the end of the meeting Jack went back to his office.

Could Bill get cooperation with his boss? Jack hoped so. He had committed himself now in an act of self-preservation.   Not knowing how long it would take them to come to an agreement, Jack new he had to start formulating a plan right now. He took out a writing pad and wrote down information he would need. A review of the information he accumulated on Vladimir/Gregorie was at the top of the list. Another thing that needed to be checked out is Bill's idea that Gregorie and Tanya were connected to terrorists. The phone rang and he was summoned to his boss's office.

Chapter 9

Cooperation

"Good morning, Ella."

"Morning, Jack."

Jack stood at her desk while she checked with her boss. He had never seen her preening at her desk and yet there was never a hair out of place or a mar in her makeup.

"He's ready."

Jack admired Connor Brooks for his directness. He was a straight talking man who told it like it was, could be trusted and was objective in his criticism. Not attributes that would have opened up opportunities in the diplomatic or political world for him. Jack hoped this was one of the times the Department and the CIA currents were flowing on attracting magnetic poles.

"Your past caught up with you Jack. You had quite an eventful weekend, it seems. I talked with a Bill Thomson this morning. He thinks your past experience could be useful in containing some terrorist plot. What's your take on the situation?" Connor moved back in his chair and folded his arms.

"I was reluctant at first, but after the attack I think it's a matter of survival. I developed a lot of information on this man, now named Gregorie, and it could help to track him down. Gregorie is bent on taking me out, so in that sense I'm good bait."

"There would be considerable absences from the office. Do you think your assistant Caleb could handle that?" Connor asked.

"Yes." Jack sighed with relief.

"Then that's it. You will maintain your position here as cover and in your absences Caleb will be in charge. Is there anyone in the office you think you might be utilizing?"

"Todd, he's the best digger." This would be a great asset, if Connor agreed.

"I will inform him of the circumstances. No one else is to be involved." Connor leaned forward with a steel gaze enforcing his remark.

"No one else." Jack did not expect this kind of support.

"Remember this is a temporary condition. I hope you don't get any ideas about returning to your old job. You're good at what you do and you're needed here."

Chapter 10

Cacti Growers

After work Jack took the same Metro line he used to commute. When he heard the familiar "Doors opening" at Tenley town Station, he got off and went to the escalator ascending the cavernous opening and flowed with the cool updraft to the street. The American Association of Cacti Growers was located a block from the station. He walked into the three storied, red brick, office building and stopped at the directory in the lobby.

On the second floor he entered the office identified as the AACG and was greeted by a receptionist who suggested he have a seat while she announced his arrival. Probably because he was back in a CIA environment, and the fact the receptionist had the build of a wrestler, he thought that she wore two hats, as many CIA employees do.

Rachel, the receptionist, gave him the OK to go in and he stopped inside Bill's office. Pictures of cacti covered the walls. Before Bill could say anything Jack said, "I expected you to have an office at Langley, but cacti growers." A big smile and chuckle followed.

"Terrorism has changed things." He waited for Jack to sit down. "How did your day go?"

"You worked wonders. I'd thought it would take a lot longer to get an OK from Connor." Jack slightly moved his head in disbelief.

"Connor is a smart man. He doesn't want to lose you, by being cooperative with you, there's less chance of you jumping ship."

"There's no chance of that. What surprised me though, was the extent of his cooperation. He even agreed to let me use Todd."

"Todd?" Bill asked.

"Yeah, he's a great digger of information. If it's in the cyber world, he'll find it. I wanted to get him started right away, but I'll hold back until Connor talks to him."

Bill opened the top draw took out three boxes and slide them across the desk to Jack. He said, "The requested Walther, a box of 9mm ammunition, and a Vault COMM 5 (Multi-function satellite communicating device). It looks like an ordinary cell phone and you can use it that way, but it is encrypted for secure contact with us and has a GPS unit. There's a manual in the box; it has many features. Your code name will be McArthur 1044."

"McArthur? Where did that come from?"

"You know, he returned, you returned." Bill shrugged his shoulders as if choosing McArthur was the most logical thing to do.

Jack smiled broadly and said. "OK, McArthur it is."

"I'd like you to meet the agent I assigned to cover your back, although now I am going to expand that function to partner." He alerted his secretary to send in Ms Burns.

When Ms Burns entered the office, Jack stood up and turned toward the door.

"Jack Dunn, I'd like you to meet Nicole Burns."

"Hi, I believe I saw you sitting at the counter this morning and on the Metro this afternoon." Jack said calmly as he pleasantly viewed the American version of Tanya.

"Yes you did. I like to keep close to my work."
Nicole said.

They both sat down in front of the desk. Bill said,
"It's only natural for you to have a lady friend, its good
cover. Nicole you can use the visiting agent's office here
and the AACG bed and breakfast accommodations."

"The Cacti Growers think of everything. No more
–get a room at the 'Y'."

Not of the same vintage as Jack, Bill let the remark
slide. "Earlier you inferred you already had something you
could get Todd started on. Do you have a plan?"

"The first order of business is to re-educate myself
with Gregorie's files and find him before he finds me. I'm
going to have Todd explore your idea that there could be a
terrorist connection; although I am not convinced it has
anything to due with the black market. Knowing his past
history and the fact he was teamed up with Tanya, I think
they contracted for a more sinister operation and the boat
show was a legitimate access to the country."

"That's possible, now, if you would bring Nicole
up to speed and call me daily with your progress." Bill
stood up and walked around his desk.

As Nicole and Jack walked to the door, Jack said.
"How about over dinner? Do you like Indian food? My
favorite Indian restaurant is not far from here."

"Great, I love Indian food."

"Then let's do it." Jack couldn't believe, because
of the CIA, he was going to have dinner with a beautiful
lady at his favorite restaurant, albeit for business reasons.

His favorite restaurant went south when Nicole, at
the wheel of her Nissan, said, "On second thought, I don't
think it would be a good idea for you to be patronizing
your favorite haunts right now. There's a small Italian
restaurant in the next block. Is that OK with you?"

"True, very true, no, that's no problem." It was reassuring to know he had a competent partner.

Chapter 11

He Made His Bed

On the second flow of a three-story tenement, Gregorie sat on a metal, fold up cot. He was looking at a very unhappy man in the mirror attached to the pine dresser. He had never been in a situation when he lost control. If a problem arose, he adjusted his plan, or aborted. Not possible in a contract with the Infidel Blood Bath. To Gregorie it was more than pride; it reached the core of his ego. That ego sustained him through his earlier years in hopeless poverty and in times of imprisonment.

He shouldn't have gotten involved with fanatics, but they needed an assassin and were willing to pay an exorbitant amount of money–even in his profession– based on his reputation. Not only did he have to deal with them, but also now due to Tanya's stupidity, he had to leave his luxurious hotel and live with them.

He heard the door open and walked out into the living area to confront them. The first one in, a dark haired man with a bony face, walked straight to the kitchen and sat down at a paint-peeling table. Gregorie and the second man, who had a face like granite, followed.

The first man spoke, "This Tanya incident was bad enough. Possibly exposing us to the infidels. For a vendetta, very unprofessional. Bad enough, but I can't believe you made it worse. I can't imagine what this man has done to provoke such madness. You have to forget about him and carry out the plan."

This humiliating address stirred anger in Gregorie that had to be held back by every nerve and muscle in his body. He learned at a young age that this energy would be better served with rational thinking and there would be another day.

"My decision was not based on revenge. I consider this man a threat to our operation." Gregorie said in a very controlled tone.

"If that's the case, I think that would be better left to us. It's a simple problem. You concentrate on your objective."

"There's also the problem of filling Tanya's role."

"I don't think it necessary for a second cab," then looking at granite face, "you can use Hadi for anything else you might need."

He had planned to use two cabs at different angles, which would have increased the chances of hitting the target, and also create confusion. Not having the second cab reduced the operation's percentage of success, but Gregorie knew he couldn't replace Tanya's skill with a rifle on such a short notice and he certainly didn't want one of those fanatics in at the crucial moment blasting away with a rifle. He reluctantly agreed—he hoped he wouldn't have to depend on Hadi for much.

Chapter 12

Going Underground

The Italian restaurant Nicole selected was a block further away from the other shops and restaurants and closer to a residential section. "Have you ever been here?" Nicole slid into the high backed booth and touched the wax covered Chianti bottle holding the candle.

"A couple of times for pizza, I like a brick oven pizza. Talk about working over a hot stove all day." He motioned with his head in the direction of the man with a long handled wooden paddle, putting a pizza in the open brick oven.

"I do too, want to get one?" Nicole asked.

"Sure." The waitress came, lit the candle, took their order for two beers and a pizza and retreated.

"So Jack, what's the background that led to all this? Fifteen years and then out of the blue someone tries to kill you."

"I was a young agent, probably about your age, operating in London—" when he finished he added, "Not good for an agent to get personally involved."

"We're not robots, we're human."

This simple statement coming from this young agent, and the sincerity it was said with, had a cathartic effect on Jack. "Do you have any questions?"

The waitress placed a steaming hot pizza on the table. "Anything else?"

"No thanks." Jack answered—Nicole shook her head.

"What's the plan?" Nicole asked.

"Meet me tomorrow on the red line and we'll go to my office. I want you to meet Todd. If Connor has spoken to him, I'll have him start looking for any terrorist connection with Gregorie."

Outside in the restaurant parking lot, Jack said, "My apartment is not far from here, I'll walk."

"I don't think that's a good idea." Nicole unlocked the Nissan.

In the Nissan, Jack said. "I think there's a little role reversal here, you walking me to my door."

"It's a different play." She started the engine and pulled out into the street.

Jack took the Walther out of the box and loaded it. "What do you carry?"

"Beretta Cheetah."

"Where do you carry it?"

"Waist band clip."

"I'll have to get one of those."

The Nissan slowed down in front of Jack's apartment. Jack reached for the door handle, but Nicole continued to the end of the street, turned around and headed back. "Did you notice the two men in the park car?"

"Yes. They're facing the path that leads to the park, Barnes and Noble, and the commercial area."

"Is that the path you'd take?"

"It is."

"What do you want to do?"

"Stop here, I'll get out and walk back. You cover. If they're looking for me, it will draw them out." Jack said.

"Is that good?"

"If we want to find them were going to have to engage them sooner or later. At least it won't be a surprise." Jack stuck his weapon under his belt, got out and walked toward the entrance. Nicole placed her weapon on her lap and shut off the lights.

At the entrance Jack heard the accelerating engine of the Nissan and turned toward the street. A man two feet from the curb aimed his weapon at him. Jack withdrew his weapon, fell to one knee and fired. He didn't know what action took the man out because at the same time Nicole's car came to a screeching halt at the curb and the man was propelled into the brushes. The other man in the car got out and began firing. Nicole returned it. The man screamed, dropped his gun, grabbed his stomach, fell to his knees, and then slumped to the pavement.   Jack leap into the front seat and they sped off.

Jack picked up his new phone and called Bill. "Another attack— just happened. Nicole was dropping me off at the apartment. Two men, not Gregorie. Dark clothes. One was wearing a skull cap. We put them down."

"I'll send agents to the scene for identification. Do you think they could be alive?" Bill asked.

"Hard to tell. I'm going underground, any room at the AACG?"

"I'll notify them you're coming. Do either of you need medical attention?"

"No, we're OK."

Jack snapped his phone closed and said. "Thanks to you Nicole I'm fine. That was a great piece of work back there. You were cool under fire. It's good to have a partner who's experienced."

"Experienced? I don't have any experience. That was my first time under fire,"

"First time! My GOD, you're good. That was text book."

Nicole flushed. "Good training that's all."

"You going to be all right." Jack was familiar with the emotional impact of taking a life.

"Right now I'm all right. Maybe later when I think about it, it might be different."

"When you do, remember to keep it in perspective. They were trying to kill us."

Chapter 13

The Bloodhounds

The next morning, after having breakfast at the AACG, they set out for the State Department. After last night's incident his habit of riding the Metro to work was out of the question. Bill told Nicole where to take her car to have it repaired—bullet holes and dents— and after they went to Jack's apartment building and retrieved his car.

Jack parked in an underground garage and they walked a short distance to the State Department. Having driven his Audi and smelling the cut grass in the park for the first time this year, Jack thought it would be more natural for him to be heading for the country or seashore. He couldn't rule out the possibility that Nicole may have brought on his daydreaming.

"Todd, this is Nicole Burns." Todd got up quickly and when he saw Nicole one hand when up to his hair and the other to adjust his pants. Jack had never seen Todd so self-conscious.

"Hi." That was all he got out.

"Todd, has Connor spoken to you?" Jack positioned a couple of chairs around Todd's computer station and they all sat down.

"Yes. He said that you were on special assignment and that I was to do some special work for you and that it was very confidential. He said that included not discussing it with other employees. What I don't understand is that I work for you now. What's the difference?"

"I've been assigned to work with an outside agency on a project. Nicole works for that agency and we're going to be working together. Now that Connor has spoken to you, you're on the team."

Todd lifted his head and in a serious tone said. "Your not leaving here, are you?"

"No, it's' a temporary assignment." Jack briefed Todd on the circumstances that led to this temporary assignment.

"Crazy man. That's some serious business." Todd had the look of a runner at the starting block.

Nicole looked up at the video games and Star Wars posters on the wall and said. "This is the big game Todd and you're the man to do it."

"I'm on it, where do you want me to start?"

"I'd like you to do some digging on a Tanya Slutskaya and Gregorie Yaroker, ex KGB." Jack replied, "They're here representing a Russian boat manufacture displaying at the Southeast Boat Exposition. They've been involved with black market weapons in the past. I want you to check and see if you can find a terrorist connection."

Todd turned to his screen and started tapping with his fingers. Jack and Nicole got up and headed for Jack's office. Before Nicole left, she touched Todd on the shoulder and said. "Good hunting." That touch ignited a rocket into the cyber world.

Jack and Nicole went to the lounge and took their coffee to Jack's office. Jack set his coffee down and turned on his computer. Nicole pulled up a chair next to him and asked. "Are you going to get everything you need from the files?"

"I think so and it will also jog my memory. " Jack punched in his new code—Mc Arthur 1044— and waited for access. "Even professionals with all their planning and discipline are human. They have their habits; their little quirks, family visits, vacations, night life, which can help find them."

"Is that how you tracked him down?"

"Actually it did lead to preventing the assassination. I had been researching Vladimir, as he was then called, and I discovered he was in London. After that I kept a close watch on him which in turn revealed the assassination plot." The first records came up on the screen with an old picture of him. "Let me introduce Vladimir, alias Gregorie Yaroker."

"He not a dangerous looking man, he wouldn't stand out in a crowd, although there is something evil looking about him." Nicole said.

"Oh, he's evil all right. He has plenty of acts to prove that." Jack scrolled the screen to the first in a list of assassinations credited to Gregorie.

"One time the victim was in a house with a good security system and had bodyguards when he left his house. Gregorie used the sewer line and snaked a five pound cylindrical bomb into the house to a spot underneath the victim's bed."

"The sewer line. Yikes!" Nicole shook her shoulders and head in disgust.

"He'll do anything to get the job done and he's very creative. That's what makes him such a dangerous man."

Jack scrolled down to the next one. "Here's one when he posed as a chimney sweep and hung a bomb in the victim's chimney. That night, when the victim sat by the fire, with his nightly cocktail, a remote control ignited the bomb. The investigation turned up two dead chimney sweeps he had used as accomplices. He'll kill anyone to get the job done."

"What do you get when reviewing cases like this?" Nicole asked.

"His M/O. It helps you anticipate his moves. You have to think like he does, and in these cases it ranges from keeping a distance from the victim to the up close and personal." Jack scrolled down to another file. "Here, let me show you. This is an example of situations when the victims are too hard to get to and then he'll do it right out in the open. In this case, in Paris, he found out the victim like horses and when he finished his evening jog in the park, he would go up to the sightseeing carriages stationed at the park entrance and give the horses a pet and treat. Gregorie, disguised as a carriage driver, shot him in the back of the head with a low caliber bullet and threw him in his carriage. There was only one other carriage there and Gregorie shouted out to him in French that this man had too much to drink."

Nicole sat back in her chair and said. "Even with all this information, how is it possible to prevent an assassination if you don't know the target?"

"You have to rely on all the intelligence sources to predict the target and an event that would make the target particularly vulnerable. When you get that and a Gregorie type in close proximity, the red flag goes up. Basically that's what Todd is doing now. Meanwhile we'll look at Gregorie's character profile to see if we can find him using any of his habits." Changing the screen, Jack went on. "This is a profile I made on him."

"Confirmed bachelor. Does he like girls?" Nicole asked.

"Yes, but he has some quirky habits."

Reading the category under entertainment Nicole expressed her curiosity. "He has a wide range of interest. Opera to strip clubs."

"Opera is almost a religion with him and he goes to strip clubs to relieve his stress, usually before or after a hit."

"Is that where his quirky habits come into play?"

"Oh yeah." Jack continued to scan through the file.

The scanning was interrupted by a call from Todd. "I found something cool that you might want to look at."

Nicole and Jack joined Todd at his computer. Todd explained, "I found information that Gregorie attended a convention of the International Brotherhood of Butchers. He is also listed on their membership roster."

"Are you serious? Butchers? If you are, it's certainly ironical. Gregorie must be president." Nicole said.

"Oh, it's real. It's an organization for meat cutters, but in today's world it could be a front. Just this morning I reported on an organization called 'Hands Together for Global Peace'. A Palestine terrorist group known as 'Infidel Blood Bath' founded it. Any confrontation with the government benefits them. They use the members like pawns while at the same time they can work under the radar."

"Any speculation?" Jack asked.

"I think Gregorie met with someone to sell black market weapons."

"Or, in Gregorie's case, some other sinister contract. Do you think it's a front organization?"

"I'm not sure. It could be a situation when the bad guys join a legitimate organization and use it as a cover to do their business."

"That's interesting," Nicole said.

Turning to Nicole, Todd asked, "What?"

"Both groups have the same initials, IBB."

Jack stood up. "Good point. See if you can make a connection."

Outside Todd's office Jack asked Nicole, "How about some lunch?"

"OK, but what about Todd?"

"You couldn't drag him away. I'll have it brought in."

Chapter 14

Collecting the Pieces

After lunch, Jack and Nicole met with Bill at the AACG. In a secure workroom they sat at a table surrounded by a bank of computers and communicating equipment against the walls. A large monitor hung from the ceiling.

Jack told Bill about Todd making a connection between Gregorie and the International Brotherhood of Butchers.

"That's quick. You picked the right guy." Jack nodded his head in approval.

"That's for sure. Bill, can you give me a contact, or contacts that can provide information on the name of the group intercepted passing information on an operation in the D.C. area and the schedules of high level officials and visiting dignitaries for the week."

Without hesitating Bill said, "For the first information, Fran Barker. The second would be known by Jim Hawthorne, FBI."

When Bill left the room, Jack said to Nicole, "I'll take Fran, you take Jim."

Jack finished first and went to get coffee. He returned and found Nicole waiting for a fax. He said, "How did you do?"

"Good. He's sending me the information now." She picked up the fax and sat at the table with Jack.

Jack brought donuts with the coffee. Having a figure like hers, he wasn't sure if she would have any, although she did do a good job on the pizza. Maybe she was one of those people who have a high metabolism, or she burned it off working out.

Nicole reached for a donut and said. "Great Idea."

"Fran said the name of the group is 'Infidel Blood Bath'. Not much to go on, just bits of information and increased activity. No target, but enough to send up a red flag."

"Amazing, the same group Todd is tracking. Do you think they are behind the 'Brotherhood?'

"If they are I think Todd will come up with it. Now let's look at what you have."

"He sent six pages, how do you want to go about it?" Nicole spread the pages out so they both could view them.

Jack got up, went to the cabinet, and brought back some high liters. "We'll split the pages and mark the international and national officials in red. The other criteria we'll use is meetings within government facilities and those outside such as cultural events, dedications, memorial services, anything that increases security problems. These we'll mark in orange."

Nicole placed three of the pages in front of her and asked. "Why would terrorist hire Gregorie for an assassination? Wouldn't they do it themselves?"

"Not necessarily. Their objective is to strike the greatest amount of fear they can, but in some cases taking on a popular government leader, who is giving them problems, increases their morale, gives them recognition, and helps recruit. The increases in security in this country have made it harder for them to operate. Gregorie, being Caucasian, blends in better. We're not sure yet that it is an assassination plot, or just a deal in black market Russian weapons. I'm going with an assassination. In that case the target is probably a high level government official of this country, or some other. That would take a degree of sophistication and experience they might not have operating in this country."

Jack finished marking and opened a notebook. Nicole slid her papers over to him. He said, "OK, let's see what we have. We'll look at the red list first and see if we can narrow it down."

Jack read the list. "I think these stand out: The British Prime Minister is meeting with the President, the Secretary of State is meeting with the Egyptian Foreign Minster, a Pakistan minister is meeting with the senate budget committee. The Secretary of Defense is meeting with the Israeli Minister of Defense." He stopped and looked up from the sheets. "Not many.'

"Why those?" Nicole asked.

"I'm trying to pick out those people who would be the most important targets for Palestinian terrorists. Of course the biggest one would be the Israeli Minister of Defense. The problem for them would be the locations and high security surrounding his meetings. Let's go over the orange list."

There were many functions listed. The only one with a high profile official was the Secretary of the Interior giving a speech to an environmentalist group.

"There it is. What do you think?" Jack looked at Nicole. "Think like a terrorist.'

"The Israeli Minister of Defense jumps off the page. The next one is the Egyptian meeting. They probably consider them traitors for having anything to do with us."

"Let's put it aside for now and keep on looking." And that's just what Jack and Nicole did for the rest of the afternoon.

Chapter 15

Close Encounter

Bill returned to the workroom when Jack and Nicole had just finished their evening meal, he said, "We got ID's on the two men that attacked you. Their names were Fahid and Kalil, both were connected to the IBB and have been in this country legally for years. Anything new?"

"Not yet."

"Let me know if you come up with anything, or need any help. I'm leaving for the night."

"Have a good one." Jack turned to Nicole. "It's time to check the opera schedule."

"Oh! We going to the opera? I'll have to change."

"No, but you'll see some entertainment before the night is over and your dressed just fine for that. Actually we're going to the end of the opera."

"The end?"

"Yes. It's time to search for Gregorie and we're going to visit his favorite haunts."

They made it to the opera house fifteen minutes before the curtain call. To an onlooker they looked like two tourists enjoying a beautiful spring evening. Cabs and chauffeurs lined up along the curb and waited for the patrons. Jack took Nicole's arm and led her to a column at the side of the entrance.

"We'll stand here. The swinging door will block his view," Jack said, and then positioned Nicole so she looked at him and he could scan the exiting crowd over her shoulder.

"No luck." Nicole said when the theater empty out.

"A long shot. Now let's look at the seedy side of his character."

"We're going to a strip club?"

"Yeah, it's called Fantasyland, and it's a lot more that a strip club."

Fantasyland was filled with fantasizes. Dim lighting covered most of the inside with the exception of spotlights focused on a keyhole shaped stage where a performer undulated around a brass pole.

The waitress left with their order and Jack scanned the tables around the stage. He paused and focused his attention on a table in the first row at the far side of the room. His body tensed and he said in a low voice, "Look to the far end of the stage where the lap dancer is performing. It's a dark area but the moving spotlight illuminates the table intermittently. That's him."

"Unbelievable," Nicole said, "what luck. You sure? He left with the dancer. They went through those curtains."

"That's one of the special services provided by Fantasyland."

"How're we going to follow him?"

Jack waved his hand at one of the dancers. "The same way he did."

"What about me?"

"I'll tell her you're part of the deal."

"Oh, that's nice."

A few minutes later, surprised by the swift deal and agreeable to the addition of Nicole, the dancer led them through the curtains to the back of the club.

In the room Jack twitched his head at the dancer and said to Nicole. I'm going to the rest room, will you kept this lady company." Taken back, Nicole merely raised her eyebrows. There were six rooms along the narrow hallway. The stripper led Nicole into the first room on the left as you faced the back of the club.

Which one was Gregorie in? Jack knew that Gregorie would always have an escape route in any circumstance, so when a dancer and client came out of another room, an idea came to Jack.

The man passed and Jack stepped in front of the dancer. "Excuse me, I'm with the fire department doing a safety check and there's supposed to be an exit back here, but I don't see it."

"Oh, that would be in the last room on the right, number six. It leads to an alley in case of a fire. That's why we never lock that room. I think it's busy now, maybe you should wait to check it. Want some company while you wait?"

"No, I'll be fine. Thanks anyway."

Jack moved to number six and, with one hand on his Walther, opened the door slowly. The only light in the room came from a strobe light pulsating every two seconds. He took three steps into the room when the alley light penetrated the opened door. A silhouetted figure darted into the alley. He rushed to get to the door and stumbled over a scantily, leather clad woman spread out on the floor, who let out a shriek. He recovered, but by the time he reached the alley Gregorie was nowhere in sight.

Nicole, weapon in hand, came up behind Jack and said. "You OK? What happened?"

"I think they were playing hide and seek." Jack returned his weapon to his waistband. "Let's get out of here."

Jack turned southwest instead of northwest in the direction of the AACG. Nicole noticed and asked as she leaned back on the headrest. "Where are we headed now?"

"If Todd is still there, which I think he is, we're going to keep him company. Jack picked up his Vault COMM 5—he was. Nicole didn't hear this; she was fast asleep until they pulled into the parking garage.

The group huddled with coffee around Todd's computer. "Find anything?" Jack asked.

"He has definitely met with them on a number of occasions, although I can't make any connection to a black market deal." Todd brought up the latest piece of information he found to back up his statement.

"If he's living up to his habits then that visit to Fantasyland suggests he has, or is about to strike."

"We haven't heard about any incident and the only significant event is the meeting with the Israeli Minister of Defense." Jack flipped open his phone. "I'll notify Bill of the possibility."

Snapping the phone shut, he said to Todd. "I want you to quit for the day. Get some rest. We'll meet back here tonight." He turned to Nicole. "We'll do the same thing.

Chapter 16

VIP Tour

Thursday evening the group, well rested and energized, gathered again for some brainstorming. The meeting with the Israeli Minister of Defense went off without incident.

"Since the minister of defense is the strongest possibility, is there any other meeting or activity he is going to attend." Jack prompted.

"Nothing that was scheduled." Nicole shuffled the papers in front of her."

"That's all official, how about something unofficial? How would we go about finding that kind of information?" Todd asked.

"He came in on a jet. He's going to leave on a jet. Todd can you find out their departure time and destination?"

"I can with some clearance."

"Bill can get that."

Within fifteen minutes they had information that the minister was scheduled to leave for Orlando Florida at ten O'clock Friday morning. On the flight plan two children were listed. On hearing this from Todd, Jack said, "Grandpa is taking a vacation."

"Do you think it's going to happen down there?" Nicole asked.

"Could be— but Gregorie is here." Jack paused and then asked. "Is there anything else between now and ten O'clock tomorrow?"

Todd's phone sounded with the theme from Star Wars. He left the table and paced with the phone. He sat down and explained. "That frees up the rest of the night, if you need me."

"Your date cancelled?" Nicole said.

Todd's cheeks colored. "No. I mean it wasn't a girl friend. It was my friend Ben. We were going to the midnight opening of a science fiction movie. He's a security guard at the Holocaust Memorial Museum. Their giving a special VIP tour and they called him to go in early tomorrow morning.

"Short notice.' Nicole said.

"That happens. They do that for security reasons. The fewer people that know in advance the better." Todd defended his friend.

"My God, that could be it," Jack said in a manner of discovery. "Let's look at what we have here. The Israeli Minister of Defense taking his family on a vacation, the day after an official meeting with the Secretary of Defense, to Florida at ten am Friday and a special VIP tour is planned at the museum early in the morning."

"That's awesome. Part of his vacation plans." Todd jump up and high fived the others.

"What's next?" Nicole asked.

"Verifying the name of the VIP. Nicole, check with that FBI agent you talked to. What's his name?"

"Jim Hawthorne."

"See what he can come up with."

"I'm on it." Nicole left the table to call Jim.

"Now Todd, let's try to answer the big question, if it's going down at the museum, how is he going to do it? Print out a map covering three blocks around the museum."

"Gotcha."

Nicole returned as Todd left and said. "Adam Barak, Israeli Minister of Defense."

"Bingo, but as I just said to Todd, how? He's getting a map of the museum area."

Todd placed the map on the table and the three of them studied it.

"OK, let's kick around some ideas. We know the security around him will be very tight. They have eliminated the public by having him tour when the museum is closed." Jack looked at the map and pointed to a side entrance. "It's less conspicuous and would reduce the time he's exposed."

"How about a pre-planted bomb?" Todd asked.

"He has used explosives in the past, but not under such high security conditions. I'm sure that place has been thoroughly swept."

"Is it one of those cases when he gets up close and personnel?" Nicole asked.

"One step back from that. He won't be able to get too close, but he's going to be at the scene with a rifle. So let's look at the places that a sniper could get a good view of the target with the longest exposure time. ."

They spent the rest of the evening postulating different scenarios and marking possible vantage points for sniping, when they finished, Jack reported to Bill.

Chapter 17

Ideas That Pop in the Night

It was a restless night for Jack. Over and over in his mind he kept reviewing Gregorie's methods until at one point he fell somewhat semi-conscious. He awoke thinking of Paris, park, and horse drawn carriages—carriage. Jack kept thinking about Gregorie using a carriage for cover. What similar thing could be used in this situation? He pictured the scene around the museum and immediately came up with cab, taxicab.

He sprang out of bed and called Bill. Could he provide a cab and driver to pick them up in half an hour? Then he woke up Nicole, who fortunately did not have any trouble with her night's sleep.

In exactly one half hour, Jack and Nicole slid into the back of a cab—Rachel was at the wheel. The early commuter traffic was light and seeing this and the pedestrians flowing into the Metro, Jack thought about his mission today and how he would have been one of them a few days ago—worlds apart.

"Taking up the violin, or working for Al Capone?" Nicole said as she looked at a black case on the seat between.

"No, that's a sniper rifle. I picked it up at the AACG weapons room."

"Oh, that ought to be useful in a fire fight." Nicole said in a skeptic tone.

"If he is in one of those buildings, or on the rooftop, it will give us something to return fire.

"Thinking about a fire fight," Nicole said, "do you think we'll be out gunned."

"I don't think so." The answer came from a smiling Rachel who picked up a 9mm Heckler & Koch MP5 submachine gun from the front seat. "I also stopped by the weapons room."

"Good thinking." Jack said and thought, some receptionist.

"Any specific instructions?" Rachel asked.

"When we get to the museum, we'll cruise around the area. Nicole, you're going to get out and scan the area buildings, especially those we targeted last night. Rachel, you'll pay attention to any cabs in the area and get as close as you can to them—if they are parked, pull up behind them."

Jack's nerves were tense. Not from fear of the action that might take place, but the failure of not finding Gregorie and stopping him in time. If this wasn't Gregorie's plan, he didn't have any ideas where it might take place. They would have to start over. Would there be enough time?

The rising sun spread long shadows across the street. A beautiful spring day had begun. A large percentage of D. C. commuters used public transportation, which left the streets with light traffic at this time.

Rachel pulled up in front of the museum. Nicole fixed her head set earpiece for hands free communication and step out of the cab.

Jack also adjusted his earpiece and said to Rachel. "Time to ride the range. Go about a block, turn around and come back on this side of the museum. That way I can watch the opposite side and any cabs in front of the building."

After a few sweeps of the area, Jack checked with Nicole. "Where are you?"

"I've walked by the side entrance a couple of times. I think the advanced security team has arrived. They've noticed me."

"Let's hope they've been brief on our presence. Just in case they haven't, go back to the bus stop on the corner it will be less conspicuous."

Jack knew it was too early for cabs to be standing outside the closed museum, but it also wouldn't be that unusual for cabs to use that area for a drop off or pick up. He decided after their last pass around the area to stand at the curb in front of the museum. It was a good vantage point.

That's when he noticed it. "Nicole, did you see that? That cab across the street."

"Yes, it pulled up slowly and left."

"Did you see anyone get out or get in?"

"No."

"I didn't either. Did you notice anything different about the cab?"

"No."

There was something different about the cab that Jack couldn't pin point.

"Nicole. If I'm right, because of the bus stop and the corner, it would be a clear shot to the side entrance walkway from where the cab was positioned."

Nicole looked at where the cab had been and turned to face the side entrance. "Clear shot. Look, there're two limos with their left signal lights on."

"And a cab pulled out from behind the last limo and pulled into that position across the street." Jack rolled down his window. "That's the same cab. It's the windows that are different; they've been covered with a dark tinting." Jack picked up his binoculars for a closer view.

He couldn't see the occupants, but he did see the back window lowered two inches and a riffle barrel resting on it. He picked up his rifle and said into the headset. "Nicole, take cover."

The shot shattered the back window and covered Gregorie with glass. "Get out of here, quickly.' He commanded the driver.

With a look of rage Hadi, the driver, shouted, "Death to the infidels." Then he picked up his UZI and drove toward the side entrance. With one arm hanging out of the window he fired wildly.

Rachel needed no instruction she immediately moved to cut them off. Jack reached over the seat and picked up the MP5.

Nicole from a prone position at the bus stop fired at Gregorie's cab. The Israeli security people took protective positions around the minister's family and moved them in the direction of the museum's side entrance.

Gregorie rolled down the window on the opposite side of his cab, raised his rifle and zeroed in on Jack. Jack fired first. It was the last time he would see Jack. In a hail of bullets he was thrown back and Hadi slumped over the steering wheel. The cab went behind Jack's cab, swerved, crashed into the bus stop shelter, and then burst into flames.

Horror struck, Jack franticly called into his phone, "Nicole, Nicole, are you all right?"

"I'm OK."

He had to be reassured. "Where are you?"

"Over here." Nicole waved from behind a light pole.

"How about you Rachel, you OK?"

Rachel brought the cab next to the curb and stopped. "I'm fine."

"Nice piece of work." Jack picked up his phone and called Bill. Bill told him to come back immediately, so as soon as Nicole jumped in, they headed back.

53

Chapter 18

Anything's Possible

In the outer office, Bill instructed Nicole and Rachel to write debriefing reports and went to his office with Jack.

Bill pulled his chair close to the desk, leaned forward and said. "Thanks to you the minister can have a nice family vacation. Not a week since this all started. That was one helluva job."

"Thanks, but don't forget the others—they were great."

"Oh, I won't. They'll be commended. How did you bring it about so fast?"

"It was information from Todd's friend that gave us the location. Gregorie's past methods gave us a clue about how. It was a gamble with some luck thrown in."

"We could use someone with your experience and luck, as you call it, on a permanent basis. Would you be interested in coming back?"

"No. I think I'll stay where I am." Jack got up and extended his hand. "Thanks anyway."

"You sure?" Bill persisted.

"Yeah, I'm sure, but anything's possible."

Jack stood next to Nicole in the outer office as she sat at her desk doing her report. "This wraps it up. You did a great job. Thanks for everything."

"Nicole looked up and said, "I enjoyed working with you."

"Do you think it would be possible for us to have dinner at my favorite Indian restaurant— now that you don't have to mind me?"

"Anything's possible. Give me a call. I'll even let you drive."

Chapter 19

Nothing Ventured,

Nothing Gained

It had been two weeks since Jack's latest girlfriend announced she was transferring to California. He wasn't surprised. This was the third time since he lost his wife, Terry, that that had happened to him. All his relationships were with career woman and they all got transferred and suggested a long distance romance, which in his opinion, never work. Maybe there was never a strong enough bond to hold things together. He had experienced those emotions that can overcome anything. First it was Greta, then after he returned to the States, his wife, Terry.

So this Saturday night, he would go it alone and enjoy a pizza and a rented movie he picked up on his way home from jogging in the park. After pouring a Sam Adams into his beer mug, he started the movie.

Two minutes into the movie an actress came on that reminded him of Nicole. He remembered the last thing she said, "Anything's possible." He thought it strange how a normally confident man can lose all confidence when emotions get involved? Was it their age difference? Was it coming up with all the reasons she couldn't possibly want a relationship with him? Or did she already have a relationship? He didn't even know that. She must. These thoughts completely distracted him from the movie. What a coward he was. He was acting like a teenager.

He learned long ago not to speak for someone else, but emotions can dismantle rationale thinking like a drop of water hitting a bucket. Maybe tomorrow he would get up enough nerve to call her.

He rewound the movie.

It was a beautiful Sunday morning before the heat of the day could settle in with the stifling humidity. The park was well maintained especially the many flower beds. As he jogged by many of them the fragrance exhilarated him. This morning more people were using the park than he normally experienced. He crossed the wooded bridge over the pond, made the circle around the pond and maneuvered the street to the dinner where he had breakfast.

After showering and dressing he sat at the kitchen table with a second cup of coffee and the Sunday paper. His attention kept focusing on the wall phone. There was no use fighting it he had to get it out of his system. Tomorrow was here. He stood up and reached for the phone and stop just short of picking it up. It would be better to call Nicole on the secure phone that Bill had given him along with the Walther. Bill told him he could still be on IBB hit list and to keep both and stay in touch. Preventing the assassination of the Israeli Defense Minister and taking out a few of the IBB members did not necessarily shut down their organization. Jack retrieved the Vault COMM 5.

"Hi Jack, what's up?"

"I finally got up enough nerve to ask you to dinner."

"At your favorite Indian Restaurant?"

"Yes."

"When?"

"Tonight, if you can."

"It took you longer than I thought. I was actually going to call you, but things got active."

"I don't know if you're in a relationship. That held me back."

"No Jack, I was but that didn't last. You know how it is in this business. Jack I think we had more than a professional bonding on that last project. I could use a good, friend right now. You should lighten up. Age doesn't factor in friendships. To answer your question, yes, I would love to have dinner with you. Do you still live at the same apartment?'

"Yes."

"Under the circumstances I'd have thought you'd move." Nicole's voice showed her concern and surprise.

"Bill had the same concerns but I like it here. I've taken a few extra security measures. I'll see how it goes."

"In that case I won't let you drive. You live close enough to walk. I'll meet you there. What time?"

"Wow," Jack let out a sigh of relief, "Your something else—how about eight?"

"Fine."

Chapter 20

Four's a Crowd

Jack looked forward to his dinner with Nicole. She sure had a way of making a guy feel comfortable. He went over to his dresser draw, took out his Walther and stuck it into the waist band clip at the back of his spine. Next he clipped his hi tech phone to his belt, put on his sport coat and dropped an extra clip of 9mm cartridges into the inside pocket of his coat. He did a last minute check in the mirror and questioned whether he was going on a date, or off to battle. Although, he thought his date was probably carrying more weapons than he was.

Instead of moving, Jack installed more security measures to his apartment. He added more motion detectors. Unlike other motion detectors these were silent and would activate a red light on the door bell alerting him when he came home to anyone's presents in the apartment. Another addition was a custom made bookcase that he attached to the smaller, guest bedroom door. He normally used this room for a computer office room, but with the addition of a single bed it became his safe zone. Anyone coming in would never know it was there.

The shortest distance between two points is a straight line, but when you live in the world of paranoia, which he felt he was in again, but hoped not for long, the safest distance between two points is a circuitous rout. When he left the apartment he took a right away from the front entrance. This route led him to the end of the corridor where he took a left to the stair well that brought him out the service entrance at the back of the building. Passing the dumpsters, he followed the sidewalk along the side of the apartment building and crossed the street which ran in front of his apartment building.

This is where he left the sidewalk and started down the long serpentine pathway which was lined with trees. It had the effect of a mini park. People often sat on the wrought iron benches and enjoyed the well groomed grass and flowers.

From the higher vantage point you could see the whole parking lot behind the office buildings on the left and in front of all the stores and restaurants, with the Barnes and Noble being the last building on the corner. Just as he was about to descend a stairway that ended in the parking lot, he saw Nicole as she quickly pulled into a space across from the restaurant. She got out and went into the restaurant. Too far away to call to her, he simply picked up his pace and proceeded through the lot until he reached a point two aisles away from her parked car. That's when he saw a car pull into the empty space next to Nicole's car. With one rolling action the man on the passenger side dropped on the ground under the driver's side of Nicole's car. With the same swiftness he leapt back into the car and then the car backed out and moved to a positioned at the end of the lot next to the road where they had a good view of Nicole's car.

It took Jack's mind only a few seconds to comprehend what was happening. Crouching low he preceded to move between parked cars to a position just behind the suspects parked car. He sent pictures of the vehicle and the GPS (Global Positioning System) coordinates to a preprogrammed number for the collection of such information and dialed Bill's secure phone number.

"Cryptonym?"

"McArthur 1044."

"Report"

"Action taken on operative's car." There was a short delay, which Jack interpreted as the call being put through to Bill.

"Bill here, explain."

After Jack gave his report, including the sending of the location and pictures, Bill said, "Where's Nicole?"

"In the restaurant."

"I'll call the Bethesda Police and alert them to the possibility of a bomb. Keep surveillance on the car."

Jack reached back and took his weapon in his right hand while holding his phone in the other. In a minute his phone vibrated.

"Nicole here, how close are you?"

"About twenty feet."

"What do they look like?"

"The last gang we danced with. What were your instructions?" Jack asked.

"He wants to move the target. He's sending Rachel to take me back to the AACG."

The Bethesda Police car turned into the parking lot and moved slowly down the aisle and stopped in front of the suspect's car. At the same time the bomb squad located Nicole's car and move a safe operational distance away. Another police unit parked in front of the stores and restaurants and began directing pedestrians away from the area. The police officer in front of the suspect's car got out and approached their vehicle.

Farid, the driver in the suspect's car, shouted to his partner, "In the name of Allah do it."

His partner Raheem pushed the button on the remote he was holding and screamed, "Death to the Infidels."

A deafening blast and concussion knocked people to the ground and broke windows across the street. Parts of the car were blown everywhere with deadly force. People were screaming and the windshield of the car landed in the pick up truck next to Jack. Jack maintained to hold his weapon and focus it on the suspect's car, but it was too late, the diversion gave them time enough to drive away from the police vehicle, over the curb and into the street. He dropped his weapon to his side. It was unsafe to fire at the car with so many people around. Standing in a dazed condition, Jack looked over the scene and felt the enormity of the act and it brought into question the humanity of the perpetrators. Jack wasn't one to what if after surviving life threatening experiences, but when he thought about what would have happened to Nicole if she had been in her car. The feeling unnerved his whole body.

Jack's phone vibrated, He clicked it on and heard, "All'e, all'e, outs in free." He couldn't believe his ears, after all these years he remembered the rendezvous code.

Chapter 21

The Best Defense

The AACG office was closed on Sunday night along with the other offices in the building. Not to look suspicious, the operatives used an entrance at the back of the building during off hours.

Jack used this entrance and walked up the two flights of stairs to the second floor. He punched in his pass word at the back door of the AACG and went inside. The reception area, waiting area, Bill's office and the conference room were all empty. No surprise here. Jack went over to the office supply room, opened the door, stepped in, and closed the door. On all three walls shelves held all kinds of office supplies.

Jack moved a box of file folders to the side, reached in and pushed a button on the back wall. The whole room moved up one floor. This is where the weapons storage room, an area partitioned with sections for sleeping, bathroom, shower, kitchen, and lounging area were located. The long table in the kitchen served for conferences.

The half glass wall that would have been along this part of the third floor was taken out, along with the entrance similar to the second floor, and replaced with a solid wall. A unique feature was the emergency exit. In the back corner of the lounging area there was a brick chimney running from ceiling to floor with a simulated fireplace facing the lounging area. At the side of the chimney there was a narrow space between the wall and chimney. This side of the chimney was open and inside a brass pole extended down two floors to the basement.

Jack walked into the lounge/kitchen area where Nicole and Rachel were sitting at the kitchen table having sandwiches and coffee while they filled out their reports.

Nicole looked up and said, "Like to have a sandwich?"

"What are you having?"

"Chicken salad on 12 grain."

"Sounds great. How're you doing?" Jack poured himself a coffee and sat down at the table.

"OK, we didn't get to have dinner, but if we did I wouldn't be around for another one." Nicole let out a sigh and shook her head, "My God! What are the odds?"

Rachel looked up from her report, "It's totally unbelievable. Think about it. The timing of Jack coming up behind them in the act, unbelievable."

They all looked up as they heard the voice of Bill coming towards them. "You're not the only ones that missed dinner. Mind if I join you? What are you having?"

"Chicken salad." Rachel said.

"That will be fine." Bill went over made a sandwich, found some chips, pour a coffee and sat down. He told them that the suspects' car was found a block away from the subway entrance and it was speculated they used that in their getaway. The owner of a newspaper kiosk on the corner of the station entrance said he saw two men running toward the entrance.

"Do you have any idea who the group is, or why they targeted Nicole?" Jack asked.

"Yes we know the group, but don't have the answer to the why. I was going to contact you this week on something that has come up, but I think this would be a good time. Let's go down to my office. Excuse us ladies."

Bill walked into his office switch on the overhead exhaust fan and sat down. He reached into his draw, took out a cigar and said, "Do you mind?"

"No, I occasional have one."

"Would you like one now?"

"You know, maybe this is a good time to have one. Thanks."

Bill lit both cigars and settled back in his chair. "The Department of Homeland Security has the responsibly for the operations of the, Border Patrol, Coast Guard, Customs, Secret Service, Counter Narcotics, and other departments crucial to the security of the country. Lew Fredrick, the new Secretary, believes the best defense is a good offence. He is going to add a department that will be made up of teams to specifically seek out any terrorists, suspected terrorists, home grown sympathizers, or any potential for disaster they find. They will be called Disaster Aversion Teams. The teams will comprise of a leader, two operatives, and a hi-tech communication specialists. They will have a high priority classification for any information they request from any of the agencies. Jack, he has asked me to run this department and I have accepted."

"I think that's the right philosophy and he picked the right guy for the job. Congratulations Bill," Jack blew a puff of smoke in the air, "but getting back to the reason you wanted to talk to me."

"My next question needed the exposition. Will you join me as a team leader? You would be the leader of the first team; maybe we could call it team Alpha. I haven't decided on the number of teams yet. That will be done as we assess the need. As for the team members, I'll let the

team leaders pick them. You don't have to answer now.
Take a few days to think about it."

"It's amazing how the turn of events can turn your
whole life around. Just a few hours ago I was a civilian
and I was thinking how the temporary assignment had
change my life by throwing me back into a world of
paranoia and constant vigilance. I was looking forward to
the time it would fade away. Then a few hours ago the
enormity of that horrific event and the pain and injury
caused to all those innocent people just to create an escape
diversion and then to think that the target was Nicole."
Jack paused and sat back in his chair. His face became
somber and his voice on the verge of angry. "I don't have
to take any time Bill. I'll do anything I can to stop those
inhuman bastards."

Bill's face expressed his pleasure and relief of
Jack's acceptance. "Thank you Jack, you're going to be a
real asset to the department. Give some thought to the
selection of your team members and you can start
recruiting. Some preliminary guidelines are that all active
government employees will receive the same pay grade and
benefits as they are now getting. Any former full time
intelligent officers and any soldiers of fortune must sign a
secrecy agreement and have bona fides. Their pay grades
and benefits will be negotiated based on their special skills
and experience. We'll meet back here on Wednesday."

Chapter 22

We're it

There was a courier waiting in Jacks' office when he arrived on Monday morning. After showing his identification and signing a receipt, he took a package to his desk and sat down. The package contained the operational manual for the Disaster Aversion Team.

The first thing he wanted to do this morning was to talk to Conner about his decision. It wouldn't surprise him if he wasn't already informed by Bill. Sometimes he wondered if Bill ever slept.

Conner wasn't in yet so he took the time to review the manual. It was something he would have to do before he began recruiting. It was a no brainer for him, Nicole, Rachel, and Todd were the perfect candidates, but would they accept?

Answering the ring, Jack said," Yes."

"The boss has arrived and said he would see you."

"Thanks Ella, I'll be right in."

Jack went in to Conner Brooks with mixed emotions. He enjoyed his work and liked working for Conner, but at the same time he felt a strong need to do everything in his power to fight the terrorists in a direct manner which would be very satisfying. He also recognized that protecting Nicole was a strong incentive in his decision making.

"Good morning, Conner."

"Morning, Jack. Although I don't know how good it is. Bill must be an early riser because he called me this morning. That's why I'm late. Monday? This is what I was afraid of. You are the man for the job, Jack, but honestly I was hoping that maybe at your age you wouldn't want all that pressure."

"You're right about that. I sure don't need that at this stage of my life, and I love this job. I'll miss the people here and I think you and I got on real well together. I thank you for that."

"Right now I think that job takes priority. Sometimes when I see what's going on today, I think I'd like to be doing that. But on another note, do you think Caleb will be able to do the job?"

"I think so, definitely, he got experience and he a good leader. Did Bill tell you I am going to ask Todd to join me?"

The change in expression on Conner's face told Jack that Bill didn't. "Todd? No he didn't. Todd he doesn't seem to be the spook type."

"Spooks come in all types Conner—as I've recently experience."

"But the "Star Wars" type." They both laughed.

"The use of technology is a key ingredient in a good anti-terrorist team. He would be very useful, if not indispensable. I'd like to talk to him today if it's all right with you"

"I'm going to be losing two good men. This is starting to get to me. You'd better ask him before I change my mind. Why do these things always happen on Mondays?"

After Jack went over the plan and made the offer to Todd, he relaxed and waited for Todd's response. There was a delay in Todd's response, but Jack thought for a guy who came in here thinking we were going over this week's projects, he was handling it well. "I never pictured myself in a role like that. I mean me a spook. Geek maybe, but spook?"

"It wouldn't be any different than the last project we did. You did any excellent job on that and you'd received the same pay and benefits. You would be putting yourself in the line of danger, though. You know the kind of people we're up against."

"I enjoyed that last project. It was exciting. You know I work on a lot of serious stuff here, but I never know the outcome. You said there were going to be four on a team, do you know the others?"

"I'm going to ask Nicole and Rachel."

Todd's face lit up at the mention of the name Nicole, Jack would have thought he'd mistakenly said, "Cat woman."

"Awesome picks. Where would we be operating out of? Would we be expected to move out of the area?"

"According to the information that I received this morning, the lease for the AACG has been transferred over to the Department of Homeland Security. As part of the Disaster Aversion Team, Alpha team's area of responsibility will be anywhere the action takes them. Your function on the team being technical could be done at the AACG. A new computer room in the AACG will hold all the latest computers and gadgets."

"Do I get to picked any of the equipment?"

"You get to choose anything you think you need. The main purpose of this department and teams is to function in a completely independent but accountable manner. No red tape."

"After that last assignment I thought you might be leaving, Jack, I felt bad about that and I thought if I had the chance I'd go with him. I guess my wish came true. Count me in."

Knowing the bad guys must know Nicole's Identity and could be following her, he put together a meeting plan that called for Nicole to enter a restaurant near the park, a short distance from the State Department, do the switch, and continue on to the park. In this case she met him wearing a tweed newsboy cap and false eyeglasses. He was pleased with the results. It was remarkable how two small changes could alter someone's appearance enough to throw off an observer. While he talked to Nicole, Rachel would be near by covering them. When he talked to Rachel, Nicole was covering them. For them the change wasn't such a big adjustment, but Rachel did mention she would be spending less time behind a desk. Jack informed her that she wouldn't be acting as a receptionist any more. The AACG front would be run by two new employees with backgrounds in the intelligent community.

He told them both that tomorrow they could move any personal items —switch articles—whatever they would like to keep there. That the function of the AACG remained the same. It would only be used for a living quarters in times of emergencies. Bill's and his office would be there and they would hold their planning and briefing meetings there. Then he instructed them to meet at the AACG on Wednesday to launch the Disaster Aversion Team."

Chapter 23

The Launch

Wednesday after Bill's overview of the team's goals he introduced the two new AACG front employees Cheryl Roberts, receptionist, and Frank Simmons, office manger; he left and turned the meeting over to Jack.

"As a new team I think our first case will be to try to find out everything we can about the group behind the assassination attempt on Nicole. Nicole, will you brief us on what you were doing before the attempt?"

"I was following up on a tip that a man suspected of being a sleeper in this country was recognized by a Secret Service video examiner in a video of an organization called United We Stand during their rally last week. The same examiner worked on a case a few years ago when a man arrested for a disturbance at the foot of the Capital steps had fled prosecution and the resulting investigation identified him as Mateem Omar. Mateem had trained in Pakistan in a terrorist training camp run by The Islamic Jihad Union."

"Do you know anything about this group?" Jack asked.

"The United We Stand organization is a counter protest against the antiwar rally and march."

"How close did you get to this man?" Did he have eye contact with you?" Jack asked.

"I was in the same group as he was and we were standing below the podium listening to a speech."

"Did he give any visual signs of recognizing you? Had you ever seen him before?"

"No to both questions, but here is where it gets very interesting Mateem is thought to have started a cell in the U. S. with funding from IBB. The Company identified the three terrorists we took out during that last assassination attempt. They discovered that the three of them resided in a tenement house on the North east side. The picture of Mateem was shown to residents of the area and he was identified as a frequent visitor to the residence." Nicole paused and took a sip of her coffee.

"It's possible he recognized you sometime during that operation, but I can think of any time you were exposed."

"I can solve that problem for you. The studies of the enhanced video cam tapes of the area the day of the assassination attempt showed a man standing at a bus stop opposite the memorial and there is a match with the Mateem photo taken at the United We Stand rally."

"That's operational procedure for these groups, they have someone observing and even taping the execution of the operation for propaganda. There it is. Mateem was the leader of the cell and hired Gregorie for the assassination and saw you—possibly all of us—and when he saw you at the rally he thought you recognized him."

Todd shifted in his chair and asked, "Sorry to interrupt, but why would this Mateem be at a United We Stand rally?"

"Todd, I want you to interrupt any time you have a question, even if it's about the jargon we use. Now to answer your question, that's what we must find out. There is some purpose to them joining any organization, and it's not always obvious.

"Mateem recognized Nicole," Rachel said, "but he didn't have any reason to believe that she recognized him. The assassination attempt on his part seems a bit extreme. There's always the possibility that it could fail and draw attention to his group."

"I think you're right Rachel and I think that finding out what made that so important is going to be our first case as Disaster Aversion Team A."

Chapter 24

Chemistry 101

Mateem's face dripped sweat as he walked along the cracked cement sidewalk running parallel with a row of low income single family homes, except for color, they all looked the same. He could hear the noise of the children coming from the fenced in school playground across the street. The walking was one of his security habits, Mateem never parked in front of the house. Before he opened the front door his body temperature rose to even a higher level. How many times had he told them to control the pungent odor?

Five people sat at the kitchen table waiting for him. Two of the men, Farid and Raheem, functioned in the cell as soldiers. They had been trained in the use of weapons, explosives and hand to hand combat. Basil, Jermal, and Adri were home grown terrorists— the carriers/triggers of the explosives.

"I believe we have reached a critical stage in our plans," Mateem adjusted himself on the chair, "our attempt at removing a government agent failed and the spectacular results turned the spotlight on us. How far along are we with our preparations?"

Farid spoke, "The hydrogen peroxide was boiled down to a concentration of 70%. Combining a 70% mixture of 70% concentrated hydrogen peroxide and a 30% mixture of flour we now have 200 lbs. which would be the equivalent explosive power of 160 lbs. of TNT."

"What is the shrapnel you are using?" Mateem was never trained for bomb making; although curious about the process he never visited the foul smelling makeshift bomb factory in the basement of this house.

"Screws, bolts and nails taped to the outside of the plastic containers." Raheem answered.

"Is that amount powerful enough to do the job?" Mateem asked.

"For people yes. Divided in three packs and spread out through the crowd there would be large casualties."

"Farid and Raheem, you will suspend the bomb making operations. Can you have the backpacks prepared tonight?

"Yes." Farid replied.

"Basil, Jermal, and Adri, You will take your packs to the safe house, lay low, and wait for the signal to proceed to the target area where you will spread out among the crowd. Now go to the basement and wait."

The three got up quickly and went down the cellar stairs. Turning to the remaining two, Mateem said, "The recent activities have exposed a threat by the same people who prevented the assassination of the minister. Their activities must be stopped before they interfere with our mission. Farid, does this Jack Dunn live at the same address?"

"I don't know."

Mateem stood up. "I want you to clean up this house—no evidence left behind—find a new safe house and verify Jack's address. He must be eliminated."

Chapter 25

Bad Hair Day

Nicole entered the supply closet and elevated to the second level of the AACG that they now referred to as the "dorm". Carpenters had replaced the sleeping area partitions with walls making three bedrooms with doors. Nicole entered Jack's office and placed a file folder on his desk. She sat in a chair and asked. "Where do all the carpenters, electricians and plumbers go—or come from—when their called to do these secret projects?"

"That's a good question. I've wondered about those special mysterious clean up teams who are called at all times of day and night. I was disappointed about our dinner plans being interrupted, although I wouldn't have it any other way. It was a stroke of luck—that's for sure."

"In our business you have to get used to it. I'm sure glad it turned out the way it did. Maybe we can sneak in good movie some time." Nicole pointed to the folder on the desk. I put the details in the report, but in summary, after the rally I followed Mateem—hoping to get his address—but lost him after he left a Beauticians Supply Company. He was in there about twenty minutes.

"What was the name of the company?" Jack asked.
"Norton's."
"We'll have to check it out." Jack made a note.

"I did. It's owned by Clyde Norton. It seems a legitimate business. Clyde was a beautician and went into the supply business about ten years ago."

Jack crossed out the last note and made a new one. "The question is why Mateem went there?"

"I don't think it was just because he was having a bad hair day." Nicole answered.

Jack looked up and saw Rachel walking by. He called to her, "Rachel."

Rachel came into the office. "Yes."

Jack held out two sets of keys. "These are for our two new acquisitions. One's a van the other is an SUV. They're in the parking lot would you check them out and have any changes made you think necessary."

"I'm on it."

"That's cool. I think this is going to be a well funded operation." Nicole said.

"You're tough on cars, Nicole."

"Well, I'm not a librarian."

"That's for sure, and neither is our nemesis, Mateem. My thinking is that the clue to why Mateem went there will be found in Norton's records."

"Specifically?" Nicole asked.

"Customer data base, invoices, shipping records."

"How will we go about obtaining them? Could a Homeland Security warrant be used to obtain them?"

"It could, but I'm sure it would take time and possibly alert the bad guys. We'll use the old fashion method. Todd's setting up his equipment, asked him to come in."

"How's the set up going, Todd."

"Awesome, I got to order from some hi-tech catalogues that I only dreamed about. Tom, from computer central, is setting up the programs I'll need for priority access to any intelligence agency. He's also told me about some new gadgets. He's the man."

Jack raised his eyebrows, turned to Nicole and then back to Todd. "We were just talking about that mysterious group of technicians. We need to get into a company that Nicole saw Mateem enter and leave after about twenty minutes. The getting into is not the problem and I think I know what records we need. This information is probably all on their computer, but how do I get to it not knowing the passwords, and what would you need to work on getting the information?"

"Companies all have to have a back up file system. It's good practice for a company to have a set of files off location in a secure place. They use external hard drives like Maxtor for this purpose. Periodically they hook up a new one and store the old one. Now, it so happens there may be any easy way. I used to work in a shipping room when I was going to college and it's there you will find the hard copies of their shipments, bills of lading, and packing slips. These are usually printed on matrix systems using perforated paper and are in fan folded stacks. They usually cover the fiscal month their working in. The disadvantage is that if you take these their absence is evidence of the theft."

Nicole said, "Could they be photographed? Maybe we could learn something by just reading them. We do know the date Mateem was there. It would be easy just to photograph the records for that date

"I like the idea—the simpler the better." Jack said.

"If you go the computer info route, my friend Tom told me about a new portable gadget that you can connect to the external hard drive and transfer the information to the unit. You would bring this back and I could hack it." Todd was enjoying being part of the team strategy meeting.

"I think we'll try the simple method first." Jack looked up and saw Rachel walking by the office. Their eyes met and she raised the keys in one hand and with her other she gave him a thumbs him up. He motioned for her to come in.

Rachel pulled up a chair and joined the others. Moving her chair a little closer she said. "Where do you want the keys kept?"

"Make two copies, one for you, one for me, and the other to be kept in the dorm. Rachel, tonight we are going to be uninvited guests at Norton's Beauticians Supply Company. I hope you've kept up with your locksmith skills?"

"I'm up to date."

"Good. Todd, I'm going to ask you to go with us tonight because I want you to gain experience in the clandestine side of our work and if I find we have to go the computer route, you will be available. Rachel you will drive the van and do the entry work. Nicole you will do the photography work. Do you have the camera equipment you think you will need?"

"Yes."

"Their security system will have to be checked and I'm sure there will be some security cameras somewhere, let's make sure we're all blacked out. Nicole, you can show Todd how this is done."

"That's it then, we will leave at twelve."

Chapter 26

Team's Night Out

At twelve, Jack was the first to arrive at the van. Rachel was next; she tossed a bag in then jumped into the driver's seat. Looking at Rachel in her black jump suit with all the bulges, Jack felt comfortable that if there was any unexpected trouble—like world war three—they were prepared. When Nicole slithered through the sliding van door, Jack thought, actually, she does resemble "Cat woman".

Todd climbed in and Jack asked. "How did you get that spiked hair under that watch cap?"

"Nicole can do anything."

"Did you bring your new gadget?"

"I did."

Rachel had just finished informing the others on the new additions to the van when she asked, "Is that the Norton building, Jack?"

"Yes pull over for a moment. Todd you switch with Rachel. Normally, in this type of operation we would try to get in with the least amount of outside exposure. I'm going to take an exposure risk because of the assassination attempt on Nicole. Somebody had been watching her, so the three of us will be dropped off at different spots around the building. Signal if you see any activity and move to the back of the building's loading and shipping door entrance. Todd, after you drop us off, you will park on the opposite side of the street facing the front of the building. You'll be the look out. Keep your radio on and signal if you see anything."

The three stood outside the shipping door entrance. The smell of diesel fumes and oil permeated the air. Because of its raised level, the shipping dock allowed the trailer trucks to back in and unload. To the right of the shipping office entrance door there were three large overhead doors used to load the trucks. Rachel reached in her bag and took out an electrical device that looked like a stud finder. She used this to scan the door. It would pick up any low current electric power used in security systems.

It did. "It's alive. I'll check the overhead doors." She reached down to see if she could lift the door. Jack and Nicole added some more power and the door lifted about ten inches before it came to an abrupt stop.

"A padlock is used in the track to prevent the door from being opened. Someone didn't put it low enough," Rachel said. Effortlessly she went under the door. Jack slid her bag through and then he and Nicole followed—it wasn't as effortless for him.

Once inside they split up, Jack went to the front office and Nicole and Rachel went to the shipping office. In no time they were looking through the reports Todd described. When Nicole found the date she was looking for, she took photographs.

Jack returned to the shipping office. Rachel said, "What did you find?"

"They use an external hard drive. It's next to the computer. Are we going to have to use it?"

Nicole answered, "No, I think we got every thing we need."

Jack spoke into his radio. "We're ready."

He heard. "I'm on it."

The three sat huddled around Todd's computer. Todd scrolled through the shipping records and packing slips for the date Matteem visited Norton's. The most obvious thing that came to their attention was the fact only one order was picked up and it coincided with the time Nicole saw Matteem. The name of the company was Red Carpet Beauty Saloon.

"Nicole, where did Mateem park when you were scoping him?"

"At the back of the building."

"Did you see him loading anything in his car?"

"No, but it's possible. There was activity going on and I didn't always have a visual of the car. After seeing him go into the building, the last visual I had of him was in the driver's seat."

Jack addressed the group. "This Red Carpet Salon appears to have a chain of stores. There are five orders for them and each has a different store number, but all have the same Post Office box number as a billing address. Todd, print the orders and packing slips. While he's doing that we'll move to the table where we can view them and have a snack break."

They all place their snacks and drinks on the table. The selections seem to reflect the diverse nature of the group itself. It included a smoothie, a Slim Fast diet bar, an English muffin and, when Todd came in and set the information on the table, a bowl of frosted flakes.

After the information was passed around, Jack said, "The items all appear to be beauty products: the usual hairspray, shampoo, conditioners and peroxide." The word peroxide struck a nerve in Jack, Nicole and Rachel. Todd didn't have the kind of experience that would send up a flag at the sound of peroxide.

All that came out of Nicole was, "Hydrogen peroxide."

Jack said, "It's interesting that all the other items are ordered in different amounts, but the amount of peroxide is the same for each salon and it looks excessive to me. Todd, I want you to check out the Red Carpet Salon and then do some research to find out if the amount would be normal usage for a salon. With this information we can get a warrant to find out how long this has been going on. This may be a normal usage, but adding Matteem and hydrogen peroxide to the equation makes it unlikely."

"Is this the regular peroxide you can buy in stores? Is it dangerous?" Todd asked.

"It is, but the commercial product has a larger percent of hydrogen and it's used in bomb making. The peroxide has to be more concentrated and mixed with flour. They set up makeshift bomb factories usually in low income neighborhoods where their not so likely to be turned in because of other illegal activities in the area. It was used in the terrorist bombing of the London subway. My God, we're on to something here. We'll meet here tomorrow and go over all the information we have and all the information on our previous scrap with the IBB. We have to find Matteem."

Chapter 27

Now I Lay me Down to Sleep

Jack reached for his apartment door handle and froze. The small red dot on his door bell was on. Someone was in—or had been in—his apartment. He took out his weapon, opened the door slowly and dropped to the floor. On the floor he scanned the room. Satisfied that no one was immediately visible he closed the door with his foot and on his hands and knees crawled into the bedroom. Nobody visible there. If no one was here they must have left me a present. Where? Most likely spot—under the bed.

The bomb was attached to a slat under the bed. Closer examination showed a remote device connected to the bomb's detonator. Somebody watching from the outside would be looking for a signal from the room that he was there. He looked around the room. When he came in the natural thing to do would be to turn on the light. That's it; the light would be the signal.

Sitting on the floor a plan came to him. Fight a remote with a remote. Jack crawled over to his closet where the Christmas decorations that he set up on his patio were stored. Two extensions were needed to connect the light next to his bed to the outlet next to the patio sliding door. The light was plugged into the extension. On the other end a heavy duty external remote was plugged in to the extension and then the remote was plug into the outlet next to the patio door. At this location it should be possible to activate the light from the sidewalk or road running along this side of the apartment.

Jack left the apartment in a different jacket and a hat pulled down to his eyes. The Walther rested in his jacket pocket. Parked cars lined the street on this side of the apartment building. He scanned the bushes and cars—nothing. At a point below his patio and bedroom window a figure moved in a parked car. He moved in back of the car behind the one he saw the movement in and stopped at the driver's side door. The decision was made, he activated his remote. The bedroom light went on.

A man stepped out of the car in front of him with a remote in one hand. In the process of pointing the remote at the bedroom, he saw Jack. Instantly he recognized him, dropped the remote and pulled out his gun. Jack didn't have to drop his remote. Two shots from his 9mm Walther sent Raheem back against the open car door and then to the ground. Jack moved swiftly to lift the body back in the car.

"Cryptonym?"

"McArthur 1044."

"Report"

"Send in the magicians. Bomb squad apartment, body in car parked on the street." After giving the car description and license number, Jack went back to the AACG.

Chapter 28

Capturing the Moment

Jack had a late start getting to sleep, but woke up at his usual early time and considered going for a morning run, but with good reason ruled it out as too dangerous. He showered and went into the kitchen for breakfast.

Nicole's cheerful greeting startled him. "Good morning, want an egg with that."

"That would be great. I didn't know you were here, although under the circumstances it was good idea."

"And I didn't know you were." Nicole set the food on the table and sat across from Jack. "Why is that? I thought you went back to the apartment."

"I had a surprise package under my bed."

Nicole stopped eating. "A bomb?"

"A bomb." Jack went on to explain the events of the night and as the story unfolded the initial look of surprise on Nicole's face turned to compassion.

She reached across the table and took his hand. "Are you OK? I have strong feelings for you Jack and I don't want to lose you thinking we never had a chance to express them,"

"I felt the same way—I could have lost you."

They both stood up simultaneously. She stepped closer and said. "I don't think we should wait for the movie. We should capture the moment." She closed her beautiful doe eyes and tilted her head up. It was met with a soft kiss and a strong hug. She led him by the hand to her bedroom. Inside they embraced each other and felt the comfort and compassion of a mother rocking and comforting her child. This turned to desire and passion and Nicole dropped her robe and moved onto the bed with enticing, outstretched hands. He needed no enticement as he followed her down. Their bodies engaged and it was like two souls mixing and flowing through their bodies with tingling pleasure. In the emotional climax, loneliness, fear, and the hate in the world were replaced by love.

Back at the kitchen table having a second coffee they both turned their heads at the sound of the chute, the term they were now using for the elevator. Rachel and Todd joined them.

"Have you had breakfast?" Jack asked.

They both replied, "Yes."

"Before we begin the old business, I have some new business to tell you." Jack reviewed the events of the evening and continued, "I think this will be very beneficial by developing forensic evidence that will help us locate Matteem and the cell. I think we must raise our guard, Rachel, I think you should join Nicole and I in the dorm. Todd, I don't think it's necessary for you, but if you would like to you can."

"I'll wait," replied Todd.

"Have you learned anything about the Red Carpet Salons?"

"I have, there is no such company and the amount of hydrogen would be excessive use for one salon, let alone five fake ones." Todd also had a late night.

"I'm sure they have had other shipments, but I don't think we will have to check that now. There always the possibility the search would be leaked. That can be done later for the records."

"What about the same box number for all the salons?" Rachel asked.

"It's legitimate," Todd said, "and the post office is not far from here."

Jack leaned forward with his elbows on the table and his chin resting on his folded hands. "Nicole, Rachel, I think the first thing to do is to follow up on the PO Box lead. Set up a video cam on the box and get a warrant for opening the box.

Todd, Nicole said that they new the location of the tenement house they used on the last operation. Use this to check out information on sales and rentals in that area for the last six months. Go through all the police civil complaint reports in that area. Look for any complaints of bad odors. They're difficult to remove when you're concentrating hydrogen peroxide. Oh, another thing, check out the rally plans for United We Stand. Maybe we can discover why Matteem is so interested in them.   Any questions? No, then happy hunting."

"Before you go Boss, do you think we could update the exercise equipment?" Rachel asked.

"You can call me Jack. That's a good idea. Talk to Frank about it."

"OK, thanks Boss."

He would have to get used to it the way he did with Todd calling him the man. Jack went down the chute for his morning briefing with Bill.

Chapter 29

Reinforcements

Farid sat on the couch watching TV when Matteem burst into a safe house room in a tenement house located in an area that they typically chose because they would less likely stand out. "Shut that off." He paced back and forth in front of Farid. Farid click off the TV and sat in an upright position. The last time he saw Matteem in this state of anger was when he was addressing Gregorie about his fail attempt to eliminate Jack. "Who are these people?" Not expecting Farid to answer, he went on. "Losing Raheem is critical at this stage of the operation. I will need every one now. The three carriers, you to throw the grenade, and me to control the timing. We will need more manpower just to fend off the infidels until we complete our mission.

The least amount of contact with his superior during normal activity was the rule, but contacting him at this late stage in the operation was to be done in only extreme circumstances. Upon hearing Matteem's, voice, the surprised superior, known as Sheik, told him to report and he recorded the coded message. Fifteen minutes later the Sheik expressed his uneasiness with a call so late in the operation and said he would supply additional warriors.

Chapter 30

Tricks of the Trade

Rachel also took the chute down after telling Nicole she would be back in a minute. She stuck her head in Frank's office. "Excuse me."

Frank look up from some paper work on his desk. Good morning, it's Rachel, right? Come In."

Thank you, Frank, I have a request and Jack gave it his approval and said I should speak to you about it. It's about getting some updated exercise equipment for the dorm."

"Updated, yes that sounds like a good idea." Frank's appearance exemplified his familiarity with exercise equipment. With the exception of his short gray hair he looked like a middleweight boxer. "I noticed the updated weapons room. I was impressed."

"Did you have any intelligence experience?" Rachel asked.

"Yes, I did— a long time ago—it was during the cold war." Frank's relaxed face tightened and was replaced by a look of nostalgia.

Rachel was instantly taken with Frank. Here was someone who walked in her professional shoes a long time ago. It aroused her curiosity. "Did you have any weapons like that?"

"No, only the Marines had that kind of fire power, it was during the time human source intelligence was at its peak. They did away with that and have replaced it with satellite and hi-tech intelligence, although I think they have seen the light lately and are returning to the field operative methods of gathering info. The preferred round at the time was the .22 caliber Stinger and we were trained to use commonly available items. Improvisation saved many a life.”

“How so?”

“When you’re working in the field undercover, you can only take a fire arm that can be concealed on you, a Beretta, Walther, or tube of toothpaste that would fire a single .22 round and sometimes that wasn’t possible. So we were trained in unarmed combat and improvising objects that could be found in any natural environment: bottles, forks, tin can lids, and rope. Oh, and of course knives. Do you carry a knife?”

“Yes I do. It sounds like something out of a James Bond novel. Oddjob, with a razor disk in the rim of his bowler hat, or the lady with a poison tipped knife in the tip of her shoe.”

“I see you’re familiar with the Bond movies,” now Frank was curious, “have you trained with a knife?”

“I learned some combat techniques.” Rachel was being modest.

“Yes close up, but it’s a very effective silent weapon that can be used to take out an adversary at a good distance. I used to be pretty good at it,” now Frank was being modest, “would you like me to train you in knife throwing?”

That was like an NFL quarterback asking a high school football player if he wanted to learn some new techniques. “That would be great, I’d love to.”

“Good, along with the new exercise equipment, I’ll order a knife target and a new well balanced throwing knife to replace your combat knife that is bulkier.”

"Thank you, when shall we do it?"

"You let me know when you're available. This is going to be fun for me too. It'll bring back some memories of exciting times."

"And you will be passing on some old tricks to a new generation." Rachel couldn't wait to tell Nicole.

Chapter 31

Bad Smell

Whenever Jack went into Todd's computer room it was like he entered the cockpit of a large aircraft except for the posters of various science fiction movies and characters. "Your posters have a new glow."

Todd looked up from his screen and said. "Yeah, isn't that neat. I added a couple of blue lights."

"How you doing?"

"I've got some hits already. One was from a school that was complaining of a bad smell. Someone from the city environmental office went out to check it but they didn't smell anything and their air check was negative for any pollutants. But what did match up was that when I check out the rentals in a square mile of their last rental, there were four rentals in that area and one was across from the school."

"We'll have to check that out. Interview the present occupants and walk the dog."

Todd, with a puzzled look, turned to Jack and asked. "As in Yo Yo?"

"No, no. As in drug sniffing dog. If there are any chemical odors in that house, they'll find it. Good, now what did you find out about the United We Stand people?"

"It's a group that is demonstrating in opposition to the anti war group, which has been demonstrating in Washington this month. They're going to march from the

Washington Monument to the White House then to Lafayette Park where they will assemble and listen to speeches by a general and two senators."

"Do you have their names?" Jack asked.

"A retired General Thomas, Senator Cole and Senator Ward."

"They sound like high profile names."

"They are, some year's back General Thomas was a household name. He was instrumental in planning and executing the first gulf war and gives many speeches in favor of the action taken in Iraq and views it as an overall fight against America's enemies. His slogan is, "If not now, when? The senators are both conservative and very active in their assigned committees."

Jack folded his arms and leaned back in his chair. "Senator Cole is the chairman of the intelligence committee."

"Right on, man."

Both Jack and Todd looked up when they heard Nicole and Rachel say in unison, "We're back."

Good, gather around and lets here what you came up with."

"Not much, although the Post Master did allow us to look in the box. It took some time for him to talk with his superiors and check out our IDs." Nicole said.

"He is going to send us the video tapes covering that box. Do you think we should put surveillance on the box?" Rachel asked.

"Not now. We can do that later if it's necessary. Right now I think we have some information that might move us further along in answering the question— what's going to happen to who?"

"Did you guys come up with anything?" Nicole asked.

Jack reviewed the possible clues to finding the bomb factory. "Now let's make a scenario out of the information we have so far. Interrupt if you want to add to the scenario or propose a different one. We have identified a known terrorist, Matteem, who tried to eliminate Nicole. From Nicole's surveillance of Matteem, prior to the attempt on her life, we found out he is collecting large quantities of Hydrogen Peroxide which is an ingredient in bomb making. Now we know they're making bombs, but what's the target?

"Now going back to the catalyst of these events, which is Nicole's observing Matteem at the United We Stand rally, he is not hiding he wants to be seen, right Nicole?"

"Yes, he was actually talking to people around him who seemed to be leaders of the group."

"Now, let me add to the equation. Todd has found out that a general and two senators are going to be given speeches to this group next week. I believe we have the target, the weapon and the terrorist who will try to blow up the general and the senators. It will not look unusual for him to be in front of the podium.

"Nicole, ask Bill to arrange a man and his dog to meet us at the CVS parking lot at eight tomorrow. Where going to check out a bad smell."

Chapter 32

Another Man's Trash

Saturday morning at eight o'clock, Jack and Bill met with their morning coffee for their daily briefing. "How are things going in the dorm? Every body comfortable? I didn't' expect you to be going into lock down so soon." Bill said.

"The workmen are all done. Those guys are efficient and fast. Everybody is comfortable. Todd hasn't joined us and I don't think it's necessary. Did they find out anything about the guy who tried to interrupt my sleep?"

"Not much yet, but the crime scene people and lab are still working on it." Bill opened his draw, pulled out a manila envelope, and placed the contents on the desk. "They did find out his name was Raheem Osman." Bill slid a picture of him across the desk. "Do you recognize him from any previous encounter?"

"No, but we are going out in the field today and this picture could be helpful." Jack gave Bill a summary of the scenario they developed and the action they would take. "How did you make out with my request for a dog?"

"It's all arranged, a K-9 officer named Nate and his dog Snuffy, who I understand is the most decorated dog in their department, will meet you at the CVS parking lot. Jack if this scenario proves accurate let me know so we can alert other agencies. That would be a terrible tragedy for a lot innocent people if they pull that off."

"They would be emboldened and encouraged to increase their attacks. We got to work fast and stop them. OK Bill, I'm off to meet a man and his dog."

It was easy to spot the K-9 officer and his dog standing in the back Parking lot of CVS. Rachel pulled along side of him and Jack opened the sliding door to let him and the dog in the van. Jack made the introductions and Snuffy made his own drawing pets of approval from Nicole and Rachel.

Todd sitting in the front seat navigating with his GPS said. "This is really cool; I've never seen a dog like that in action."

With instructions from Todd, Rachel slowed down and stopped a short distance from an eliminatory school. Nicole jumped out and Jack handed her two magnetic signs that she stuck on each side of the van. Now they were riding in a van from the Environmental Air Testing Department. Nate having been instructed not to enquire as to what department these people work for, or anything about the mission, looked on with curiosity.

The task finished, Jack said, "Pull up and park across the street from the school, but not directly in front of the house." When this was done, Jack switched seats with Todd, took out a pair of binoculars and scanned the area. "Todd, is that a gas station and convenience store on the corner?"

Todd looked at his GPS. "It is."

"OK, it's prop time Nicole."

Nicole opened a black gym bag on the floor and took out a hard hat, with the Environmental Air Testing logo on it, and an orange florescence vest. She stepped out side and put these on."

Jack opened the van window and said. "I don't know why those people would need a hard hat, but it looks impressive."

Todd handed her the clip board and she was off.

Jack lifted his binoculars for another scan of the area. First he focused on Nicole at the front door of the house, when nothing was happening there; he turned to view the area in front of the school. At the beginning of the school bus pull over area there was a public bus stop. Two men were sitting there. No, it was too big a jump to think they had people watching the possible bomb factory. He turned back to Nicole who was looking in the window. She turned to the van and shrugged her shoulders.

"Rachel, you and I will go up to the house, Todd and Nate, you wait for my signal." When they reached the front door Jack said. "Nobody home?"

"Look for yourself, it seems completely abandoned."

Jack did just that and said to Rachel. "Do your magic."

They moved into the house swiftly and Jack motioned to Nicole to go up and to Rachel to go down. He went through the kitchen and back into the living room. He waited for their return and glance out the window. The bus pulled away from the bus stop and the two men were still sitting there waiting for a different bus—or not. Nicole and Rachel returned and declared the premises empty. Jack stepped out onto the porch and signaled for Todd and Nate to come in.

Inside the house the dog went directly to Nicole and Rachel with a warm greeting. With one command from Nate, Snuffy's attitude changed from friendly and playful to all business. All of them followed behind as he went through the house.

In the basement he became very excited and went from one area to another where he stood shaking with excitement. "In my amateur opinion it looks like a hit," Jack said.

"It is, and I would say the forensic people should be called in." Nate knelt down to reward Snuffy. "They cleaned up but not good enough for Snuffy."

Nicole asked, "What's this white stuff?"

The group moved to the basement wall on the back side of the building. Jack knelt down run his finger across the substance and brought it to his nose. "It's not drugs. I think it's the other ingredient in the bomb making process—flour."

"That's why Snuffy didn't react to it." Snuffy made a big impression on Todd.

"They had to move a lot of supplies in and out of here. Rachel check out the back yard. Todd and Nate, you return to the van. Todd, you'll take over the driving. Start the van, open the sliding door and be ready to leave quickly. Nicole, give the house a quick search for anything they left behind that could identify them.

Jack, Vault COMM 5 in hand, stood in the living room next to the window on the phone with Bill. He requested all the surveillance video cam tapes from the school and the convenience store as soon as possible. He was hoping the school security cams covered the public bus stop. He looked at the public bus stop—the two men were gone.

Rachel went out through the bulkhead into the backyard. She looked around and found nothing unusual. Next, she went to the side of the house where there was a kitchen door and a side entrance gate. That's where she saw the trash barrel. She lifted the cover and it was full of trash. She rolled it over to the picnic table, lifted the lid, took out a garbage bag and placed it on the table. Two dark figures flipped over the fence and landed on the ground. Rachel instantly dropped behind the picnic table and trash barrel. This action caught the eye of one of the terrorists as both of them moved close to the ground and in the direction of the house. The terrorist nearest to Rachel fired two shots from his automatic pistol at her. The other one took out his Uzi from under his jacket.

The two shots were heard by Jack and Nicole. Nicole was in the upstairs bed room and looked out the window facing the backyard. The two terrorists were on the ground, one aiming at Rachel and the other in the act of taking his Uzi from under his jacket. Nicole raised the window, and dropped to the window sill.

The terrorist, with the Uzi, had aimed at Rachel and when he heard the sound of the window being opened he turned his aim at the window. Nicole's shots came first and then Jack's sounded from the kitchen door. The second terrorist was distracted toward the action and Rachel took him out.

The three of them moved cautiously, weapons fully extended, toward the two slumped bodies on the ground. Jack said, "Let's quick strip them and get out of here." The three gathered all the items they found on the bodies and made for the side gate.

As she passed the picnic table Rachel yelled out. "The trash, the trash." She threw the bag in the barrel, closed the lid and pulled it to the van. The trash barrel landed in the second row seats and the three jumped in.

Snuffy was very excited, the barrel added to Nate's bewilderment of the whole operation and Todd drove down the street. He said, "Hey, we're in the environmental business. We're picking up trash."

Nicole snapped back, "And we got rid of some too."

Chapter 33

Smoke and Mirrors

After the team had dinner, they cleared the table and clean up the kitchen. Finished, Jack said, "It's time to roll out the barrel."

Rachel went to the supply cabinet and brought back a box of throw away plastic gloves. Todd pulled his on and said. "I feel like I'm in the hospital."

"Let's hope they prevent you from going to the hospital," Rachel said.

A trash bag was placed on the table and Jack untied the bag. Todd asked, "Is their anything special we're looking for?"

"Any paperwork that could give us information about their identity, or their plans," Jack answered, "we'll pull out. The rest of the material will be sent to forensics for their work. Speaking of forensics, I'll also send the items we retrieved off their bodies."

Jack left the group and returned to the table where he placed the items on the table. The first thing he looked at was a cell phone which he gave to Todd. "His phone records would be useful, especially the ones made today." Addressing the group, He said, "Anybody find anything interesting?"

Nicole answered, "Most of the receipts are from the convenience store at the corner, but I did find an interesting one from a company called Metro-Med. It's a retail medical supply company."

"Don't tell me it was for hydrogen." Jack said.

"No, that wouldn't raise my curiosity as much. It's for three white canes."

The group paused what they were doing and all looked at Nicole. Jack said, "White canes? That is curious. It'll have to be checkout"

Jack picked up one of the items taken off the bodies. "What have we here?" It was a folded map. He unfolded it and spread it out on the table. It showed a large scale map of the Washington DC area with hand written notes on it and a stick figure truck drawn on the Arlington Memorial Bridge. A time of nine O'clock Tuesday morning was written under the truck. "

Todd when did you say United We Stand is marching?"

"Tuesday morning."

"Maybe that's not the target at all," Nicole said.

"This is too much of a coincidence. Three days before the day we think something is going down and we are attack by two terrorists and one happens to be carrying a map of an intended target." Jack looked from one to the other to see if they too had suspicions.

"The whole thing is strange to me," Todd said, "I still don't understand there being there at all."

"It's not uncommon for terrorists to watch an abandoned operations area to see if anyone is on their trail."

"Wouldn't they have to stake it out for a long time?" Todd was still trying to make sense of it.

"No, it probably wasn't vacated that long and they have plenty of time." Jack picked up one the victim's wallet and opened it. He unfolded and placed two pictures on the table. "And this was an added incentive." The two pictures were of him and Nicole.

"I think we have a dilemma," Nicole said.

"I think we have a diversion. The way I see it their mission was two fold—take us out and prevent us from stopping them, or if that failed, plant evidence to divert us. I'll alert the other security agencies to the possibility of the bridge being a target, but we will focus on the United We Stand rally as the target."

"Jack, this may be silly, but I keep thinking about those canes," Rachel said.

"The three white canes?" Jack looked puzzled.

"Yes, I kept asking myself where I remember that from and then it came to me. The three blind mice. You know the three assassins in the James Bond movie, "Dr. No"."

"Amazing," Todd said.

"There going to use that as a disguise to bomb the rally," Nicole said.

"Very clever, Rachel, now we know what to look for and there're at least three of them. It's time to take a break. Let's put away the trash and watch a movie. Tomorrow is Sunday; we'll have a review meeting at three O'clock. Bill said we should have the enhanced surveillance videos by then. Who's going to pick out the movie?" Jack let them decide.

The three of them went to the video storage cabinet and the majority ruled. Nicole put the video in the DVD player. It was not Todd's type of movie. He said, "You know I think I'll check out and catch up with you guys tomorrow."

Rachel sat in the arm chair and Jack and Nicole sat on the couch. It wasn't long into the movie that Jack discovered it was a chick flick. Rachel decided to give up her fight to stay awake and went to bed.

After Rachel left, Nicole cuddled up to Jack. "This might be it for a while," she said.

"That's fine with me. It feels real good." Jack put his arm around her and his attitude about the movie completely changed—he was more optimistic about finishing the movie.

Chapter 34

Extra Eyes

Jack heard the chute before he saw Bill. "Hi, Bill, this is unexpected." Bill put his brief case on Jack's desk and sat down. "I'm glad you came though, I've got some things to go over with you."

"This is what brought me." Bill opened his brief case and took out videos. "These are the enhanced surveillance videos from the school bus stop area and the convenience store. The early photos show three suspicious men using the bus stop and also in the convenience store with one or two shots of another man. The last photos at the bus stop show pictures of the two men who attack you.""

"That's our man Matteem at the store, but I don't recognize the two men at the bus stop. I'll have Todd send these to Interpol."

Bill reached into his case again and pulled out other photos. "These post mortem shots of the two men who attacked you and their fingerprints might be more useful for identification."

Jack told Bill about the receipt for the three white canes and the map found on the assassin's body. "We talked about the possibility of the map being a diversion and what really convinced us that it was a diversion is Rachel's connection with the Three Blind Mice, of the

James Bond movie, they were assassins in the Movie *Dr. No*."

"That's something else; I take it she's a movie buff. Good for her."

"She's too young for the original movies," Jack said, "but I bet she has all the DVDs."

"So, you're going with the rally as a target. If that's so, all the agencies will have to be alerted to the possibility of the target being the Arlington Memorial Bridge." Bill said.

"That's it, and the Metro Police, Secret Service, Park Security and all the private security agencies will have to be notified that we will be operating in the park. As recognition we will be wearing yellow hats. There is one problem."

"What's that?" Bill asked.

"Numbers, we know three bombers will be roaming the crowd and Mateem, for whatever reason, will be in front of the podium. He's established a presence there—maybe to control the operation."

"And?"

"That's four people to cover and Todd is not trained in field work." Jack answered.

"That's no problem, I'll come along."

"You sure?"

"Why do you think I took on this job? I'd like to get those bastards too. I think I'm going to ask Frank too. You can always use extra eyes." Bill had a smug look on his face.

The three team members had gathered at the kitchen table where they were waiting for the meeting. When Bill left, Jack walked out, got himself a cup of coffee and said. "Let's get started." Jack took a sip of his coffee and waited for everyone to pull out their note pads and get settled.

"Todd, this envelope contains information I want you to send to Interpol."

"Interpol? That's awesome. Tom told me all about Interpol. Did you know Homeland Security is going to have a man working in their European office at Lyon?"

"Tom?" Jack asked.

"Yes, the computer program tech that set up my programs.

"That's good Todd because you will be using that link a lot. They have the largest data base on Terrorist in the world. Todd have you tried the cell phone blocking gadget?"

"Yes, and it works."

"What distance did you check it?"

"Ten feet."

"Check the manual for its maximum range and then test it."

"I'll be carrying it on Tuesday. Todd, I want you to stay on the information trail, follow through on the cell phone and the evidence I've given you. Your assignment Tuesday will be using the van as our communications center and our transportation. You will monitor any communications coming from the park, ours and any others you might pick up. You'll want to know what the other agencies are using for frequencies. Rig up the van to look like a TV or Radio station vehicle. Nicole and Rachel will help you set up your equipment in the van and with disguising it. "

Todd was excited about his role in the operation, but his face showed an expression of concern. "You'll be shorthanded if you are going man to man in the park"

"Bill and Frank are going as extra eyes and both have worked in the field." And then addressing the team, said, "Now, for op day our recognition code will be yellow hats, so implement them in any disguises you are going to wear. Tomorrow afternoon's pre op meeting will be a dress rehearsal. See you then."

Chapter 35

Dress Rehearsal

The team came to the pre op dress rehearsal meeting in their blend in with the United We Stand rally participant's attire. Rachel's was the most outstanding of the team. You couldn't tell it was Rachel. She had long, matted, gray hair hanging down to her shoulders and was wearing a bright, yellow, knitted hat. A brown vest covered her flannel shirt which hung outside her baggy pants.

Nicole was wearing jeans and a tank shirt with an eye-catching United We Stand logo on the front and an American flag on the back. A large pair of sunglasses covered a good part of her face and her hair was tucked up under her yellow baseball hat. A fanny pack was on each hip.

Jack and Bill, similarly, had jeans, T-shirts and yellow baseball caps.

Frank was wearing tan khaki pants, a short sleeve brown shirt with epaulets, and a flat topped, short brimmed, yellow hat that he told everybody he didn't like, but it was all he could find.

Todd was wearing his usual attire and one could say he would fit in at any type of rally. He didn't have the yellow coded hat because he would be in the van. He proudly told everybody that the van now looked like a mobile radio station unit.

Jack passed out maps of the park. "This map of Lafayette Park has been marked off into five sections. I'll take the south section, A, the area in front of the podium: Frank, you will cover the southwest section, B, Bill the southeast, C, Rachel the northwest, D, and Nicole the northeast, E."

"Do you think they are suicide bombers?" Nicole asked.

"I don't know. It depends on how many martyrs are available. In some of the other terrorist bombings they used a drop and explode later with a remote technique. That brings up an important point. If you see a backpack being placed, or in place, and the terrorist standing nearby, take him out, but it's important to communicate that to Todd. He will relay the circumstances to the rest of us and inform the bomb squad. If he has placed the bomb and is waiting, I would interpret that to mean that he is waiting for a command from someone. I am still trying to work out Matteem's role in front of the podium. He may be going to control the action from there. It's obvious that the most important targets are there, the general and two senators. Any explosions in another area would divert security's attention to that area."

"What's the march route?" Frank asked.

"From the Capital to the White House and then to the park." Jack could understand why Frank wasn't particularly fond of his hat.

"When will we interact?"

"You, I and Bill will be dropped off at the White House so we will be in the forefront of the group. We will march with the group to the park. Todd will deploy Nicole and Rachel on the north side of the park and place the van there."

Chapter 36

A Beautiful Day at the Park

The weather prediction for the day was for mostly sunny with a twenty percent chance showers and a 75° temperature. Jack timed their arrival in front of the White House to be about a half hour before the demonstrators arrived.

Jack sat in the seat next to the sliding door and gave instructions to Todd to pull over. Jack was out first and then Bill and Frank got out. In the process of closing the door, he notice Rachel seating in the back and it made him think of her this morning loading a two wheeled cart, an accessory to her bag lady outfit, into the back of the van. He couldn't imagine what she might be carrying in it. Rachel always came prepared.

The three of them watched the van take off down the street. Small groups of antiwar activists were already gathered to protest the march and when the van, looking like a radio station mobile unit, passed them they shouted and waved their banners.

In the distance the three of them could see the marches spread out from one side of the street to the other with their flags and colorful posters. Their leaders were out in the front leading the way but retired General Thomas, Senator Cole and Senator Ward because of security reasons would meet the group at the park.

It was an impressive sight watching the group move slowly toward them and growing in size until they spread out all around them. As they did at the Capitol, they sang patriotic songs and shouted out their support for the troops.

This is where they joined the marches as they started to move toward Lafayette Park. Once they started to move with the group, Frank's bearing bespoke of his military background but with all his discipline he could not hold back the enormous pride he had for his country and one had only to look in his eyes to see it. Jack was equally moved when he saw Bill take out a small flag from somewhere and start waving it. It was at this moment that the monstrous nature of the act struck Jack. There were thousands of people like this in the crowd and also terrorists who wanted to randomly kill them. Jack prayed to God they could stop them.

They all had pictures of Matteem and the other suspects that were enhanced from the video surveillance cameras. Jack made a match with the photo of Matteem just as they turned into the park. Next to Matteem was another dark complexion man who exchanged a few words with him. He was wearing a jacket. Jack thought it was a warm day to be wearing a jacket. He caught Bill's and Frank's attention and motion with his head in their direction. They both nodded with signs of affirmation. When they reached the front of the podium area, the other man separated himself and stood closer to the podium.

Todd dropped off Nicole and Rachel at their assigned areas and found a good spot right next to the park. It was not an area you would park a car, but because of the radio station logo and the occurring event he could get away with it. He turned on his equipment and contacted each team member for a test. They all check in and then he started to monitor all the radio frequencies that he was given by all the security agencies, when he was satisfied that they were being pick up, he set this on scanning and he turned on a special new unit that Tom had showed him how to use to pick up any communicating devises that the terrorists might be using.

Jack and Bill were also doing some checking. Jack was using the new jamming device Todd had been given to shut down cell phones, or any other electronic devises that emitted sound, to test it on Bill's phone. The test was successful at what they approximated at about twenty feet. He knew it could shut down, cell phones, I-Pods, radios, and walkie talkies, but he didn't know the effect it might have on the events sound system. He dismissed this as a problem because even if it did it would not be long lasting.

The long line of marchers filled the park and all the streets around it. General Thomas, Senators Cole and Ward had not arrived yet but the organizers and officials of the event had and were taken their place on the podium. The music from the band entertained the group and flowed loud and clear through the sound system.

Nicole saw the terrorist sitting on a bench. She walked by and saw him in the act of placing his backpack under the bench. When she turned, the terrorist got up and walked away—without the backpack. She followed him a good distance until he moved toward another bench. He was doing very well for a blind man. There was a person on the bench who was intimidated by this blind man waving his white cane wildly at the bench and he got up and left. Nicole walked a short distance, turned on to the grass, circled around a tree and came up in back of the bench. He had his cane in one hand and a walkie talkie in the other. She took a black jack out of her fanny pack, checked out the pedestrian activity, moved a step closer and walloped the terrorist on the head.

She called in the location of the backpack laden with explosives to Todd who relayed it to the bomb squad stationed at strategic spots around the park. The unconscious body of the terrorist was taken away by Homeland Security employees disguised as Para Medics and using an authentic ambulance as cover. To a bystander it would not be unusual for a demonstrator to drop from heat exhaustion and be taken away in an ambulance.

Rachel spotted her target reclined on the grass with his head on his backpack and surrounded by others doing the same thing. She pushed her two wheeled cart over to the area and got there just as he got up and walked away, leaving his backpack. He continued along the path until he found a bench and made his move to sit down. Rachel stayed close to him and when the two people on the bench saw these two characters coming at them they got up and left. Rachel sat next to the terrorist and reach into her cart for her thermos. She poured herself a hot cup of coffee and dumped it onto his crotch. He cried out an expletive and bent forward. Rachel directed a powerful rabbit punch to his exposed neck. Another call was made to Todd.

Bill walked along the path toward the south side of the park. A blind man was approaching him with a backpack. His cane in front of him searched for obstacles and his other hand empty. When Bill was abreast of him, he turned and placed his left foot behind the target and delivered a punch to his mid-section. He went down and Bill followed. On the ground Bill placed his knee in the target's stomach and a hand clutched the terrorist throat. He moved his head closer to simulate mouth to mouth and then lifted his head and to some bystanders said. "It must have been the heat." A third call was made to Todd.

General Thomas's introduction was met with wild cheering and thunderous applause. The message of the third take down was just delivered to Jack from Todd. It was amazing —what a team. He had kept Matteem in his sights all the time without getting too close to him to be identified. The question now was what would he do? He didn't have to wait long, at the moment General Thomas started speaking Matteem lifted his walkie talkie. The start of the speech was the signal to give his command to start the first explosion and divert the attention of the security away from the podium. The other explosions would follow. Evidently Matteem didn't realize he didn't have anybody left to command, or did he? Jack didn't' take any chances and triggered his jamming devise.

Matteem's face immediately express panic and he shook his walkie talkie, tried one more time and threw it to the ground. Jack moved in closer and saw him turn toward the podium and in a rage he shouted. "Throw it now, throw it now."

Jack turned away from Matteem and saw who he was shouting at. It was the man he saw him with early in the march. The man reached under his jacket and took out a grenade. Now Jack panicked, with both hands holding his weapon and the man in his sights, he realized he couldn't fire without risking the lives of the people around the man.

The swishing sound of the knife whirling through the air ended with a thud as it struck Farid in the middle of his back. He froze with his arm extended above his head and crumbled to the ground. His body covered and absorbed the shrapnel and power of the grenade which lifted his body three feet off the ground.

Jack looked to see where the knife came from and saw Frank—the extra pair of eyes—casually walking away. Remembering Matteem, he looked back to the last spot he was in—he wasn't there.

Chapter 37

Kudos

Jack addressed the team at the post op meeting the next morning. "I reviewed all your reports and I must say that I'm very proud of you. We left only two lose ends, the last body, and Matteem getting away. The body is no problem and we will definitely track down Matteem."

"No, the body won't be a problem because the credit has been given to the Secret Service." Bill walked up and tossed a newspaper on the table. A front page story read "Secret Service Foils Assassination Attempt on Ret. General Thomas's Life". That's good because the last thing we want is publicity. As for Matteem, Jack, your right, I think he could be a very important lead to the IBB's hierarchy."

"I can't imagine the Secret Service taking out someone with a knife." Nicole laughed.

"That Frank is unbelievable. He's going to teach me how to do that." Rachel said.

"He was the force," exclaimed Todd.

"That was unbelievable. Where is Frank?" Nicole asked.

"He's down stairs in his office." Bill said.

Thinking this needed some explanation Jack said, "Frank saved the day but he's not one for a lot of attention, you can give him your kudos later." Frank had definitely picked up some fans here.

"You did a good job too Bill." Nicole said.

Bill was a little taken with this, he said, "Thanks, I'll let you go on with your meeting." He took the chute down.

Jack went on, "Before we get into anything else, I'll tell you that I don't think we need to hunker down here any longer. I'm going to move back to my apartment today.

Nicole and Rachel, while I work with Todd on the electronic information gathering, I want you to take the pictures of all the terrorists we've encountered so far and revisit the safe houses , neighborhoods, convenience stores and see if we can get any more information on them. I like to see if connections with each other can be made. I have a feeling that the last two we engaged at the bomb factory were from a different group, if so, that could lead us to another cell."

Chapter 38

An Unwelcome Visitor

Dr. Warren Ketchum, known to his followers as the Sheik, controlled the IBB's cells within the Washington D. C. area. A small dark man with black, deep set eyes covered by small round eyeglasses. His cover is a chemical testing laboratory located one quarter mile inland from the Patuxent River. The property is surrounded by idyllic Mennonite farms and is accessible to the river where there is a docking facility and the company boat. Locals, UPS, or similar companies, deliver water and other chemicals for analysis.

Once the impressive home of a sea captain it was now the home of Ketchum Chemistry. A modern laboratory and offices were installed on the first level to carry out the legitimate operations of the company. The lower level was designed for the production of chemical weapons and accommodations for the employees. Dr. Ketchum intends to use these weapons in an attack of the Washington Metro subway system. It would produce the largest number of causalities of any previous attack by terrorists.

Dr. Ketchum, in his white lab coat, paced back and forth behind his desk and in front of the bay windows looking out across a manicured lawn to the edge of the forest. He only stopped to flick the ashes of his cigarillo in the desk top ash tray.

The failure of Matteem on the two high profile assassinations was beyond his tolerance. He was a man of science and couldn't understand such failure. It was almost impossible to control these cells. Their independence was crucial to maintaining the hierarchy of the organization, but the decisions of the leaders could not always be scrutinized for there possible flaws.

He stopped pacing and lit up another cigarillo. These cells were not always staffed with skilled members. A few cells had the true believers who were willing to be martyrs; the others, of the home grown variety, were not as fanatical, or as well trained. The Dr. was fortunate to have members in this unit who were of the true believer type, like himself, and had been sleepers in this country for a long time.

The failed assassination attempts were one thing, but to jeopardize his operation was inexcusable. His own cell member made the mistake of calling him from the bus stop. He could no longer be punished for his act of stupidity, he was dead, but Matteem a man who should have know better and was actually on his way here, without it being authorized, would have to be dealt with. He actually called again to tell him he was on his way.

Dr. Ketchum placed his cigarillo in the ash tray and pick up the office intercom. Sanjay, his assistant, reacted to the flashing light on his desk. "Yes."

"I want you to meet Matteem at the reception desk when he comes in. Tell him I will meet him in my lower level office and that he will have to be decontaminated before he proceeds into the sterile production area."

Puzzled Sanjay asked, "Is that necessary if he's just going to your office?"

"No but if he has to leave this world, why not use him for a test. It will probably be the most useful thing he's done in quite a while."

The "decontamination room" was also an area they used to test their chemical weapons on animals. Now Sanjay understood, he nodded in compliance and said. "It will be carried out. I'll make the necessary arrangements."

"Welcome, Matteem, I've been instructed to take you directly to the Dr. who is working in his office in the lower level. How was your trip?" Sanjay turned and lead him to the stairs leading to the lower level.

"It was a long trip and it's so remote I had trouble finding it. The people I asked in the area knew nothing about it."

Sanjay cringed at this statement and was glad that the Dr. didn't hear it. "That's a good thing— isn't it?"

"Oh, yes of course. This is quite a modern facility you've got here. I had no idea."

Sanjay stopped in front of a room that looked like a large sauna with a small window in the front door. He said, "Take your clothes off and step into this room. Everyone entering the lower level must be sterilized."

"Does that include you?" Matteem asked.

"No, I'm not going in the production area."

Matteem looked to the right and saw the production facilities and left to an area that held offices and accommodations. He looked in the window and saw a video camera unit on the ceiling. He pointed at it and said. "To expose my body to others is against my beliefs."

Sanjay leaned over and looked in to view the camera. "Oh, that's only used in some of our other experiments," Sanjay walked over to a locker and brought back a robe which he handed to Matteem, "here take one of these lab coats."

The word experiment was not the right word to use. Perspiration beaded on Matteem's brow. His eyes tightened and he looked around with the uneasiness of someone walking down a dark city alley at night expecting someone or something in the shadows to leap out and attack him. He undressed and used the lab coat Sanjay had given him and stepped into the room. Sanjay look in the window and smiled while his unseen right hand turned the lock on the door.

The Dr. had already turned on the camera and was watching Matteem on the screen, when Sanjay joined him. "He looks nervous. Do you think he suspected anything?"

"Yes, I think he did. I think it was that primeval inner alarm system that was warning him, but he fought it off with the false belief that he was among comrades in arms."

They both watched as the nervous Matteem was waiting for something to happen. The Dr. activated a switch to start the process. In another area a technician started the process that would send the deadly agents into the room and record all aspects of the experiment from the number of units delivered to the first and last affects on the body of Matteem.

Dr. Ketchum and Sanjay watched as Matteem's eyes bulged and broken blood vessels appeared on his body. His body went into convulsions and he made desperate attempts to breath. "It won't be long, Sanjay, and this will be the same death that will come to thousands of Infidels."

Chapter 39

Everybody's Gotta be Someplace

It had been six days, four work days and the weekend, since the Disaster Aversion Team avoided its first disaster as a team. The team had collected human and electronic intelligence for their new data base on the IBB. The information trail started with the failed assassination attempt on the Israeli Defense minister to the present and this Monday morning they would analyze what they had.

"Todd what do you have from Interpol on the information you sent them?" Jack started the meeting.

"Some success, but nada on the three bomb carriers." Todd shuffled the reports in front of him.

"They're undergoing interrogation now, maybe we will end up with more than their pictures and fingerprints—and of course DNA. What about the others?" Jack asked.

"Matteem. Farid and Raheem are all in the Interpol data base. All three at various times were stopped trying to cross a border illegally and Farid and Raheem have records for minor criminal activities. All three can be placed at different times to places where there have been attacks by the IBB." Todd slid the report over to Jack.

Jack reviewed the papers in front of him. "That leaves us with the two that attacked the team at the bomb factory, anything on them?"

"Yes, Interpol has identify them and they also have information which was gained through interrogation that these two men, Karem Yahya and Habrid Ibrahim, were specially trained combatants and were usually used to protect someone higher up in the chain of command, or an important plan that was in progress," Todd took a breadth and added, "and these guys were sent to take you out. It's hard to believe this is real. Here I'm communicating with Interpol and it's about two guys from about four thousand miles away who are over here trying to kill us."

"That's the reality of it Todd and many people haven't come to terms with it."

Nicole said, "Our investigation from the human information and the video surveillance showed that there was a connection between the bomb carriers, Farid, Raheem and Matteem but none with the two at the bomb factory. You new they were different, how could you tell?"

"It's hard to put a finger on it, but I think most of it is instinct, but it is also a trained eye. They looked different than the others we've encounter so far and the way they moved and handled their weapons had a lot to do with it."

"If that's the case, that they are different and maybe not connected with Matteem's cell, why would they be called in?" Rachel asked.

"It could be that Matteem lost too many members to concentrate on the execution of his plan and fend us off at the same time and we were getting too close to finding him. We know from experience that these cells are small. If he was desperate and had to call in help from some other cell, this would be a good link for us to follow, if we can make the connection."

"Now we have plenty of information on our adversaries, but the question again is where Matteem is? What did you get from the cell phones?"

Todd's answer was interrupted by Cheryl, the receptionist, who said, "Bill sent up some coffee and bagels to stimulate your thinking."

"That was very nice of him. Send him our thanks." Jack reached for a bagel.

The others did the same and when they finished Todd tasted the coffee and proceeded to answer. "There were two cell phone records to investigate, one from Raheem Osman and the other from Karem Yahya. Raheem is the one who tried to blow up Jack and Nicole and Karem is the terrorist at the bomb factory. Karem made a call and it was received by a number in a roaming mode in a remote area of Maryland and in fact could have been on the Patuxent River. The information on the owner of the cell phone is false. I asked the wireless communications monitoring people to search for any other call to that number in the DC area and they came back positive."

"When was that?" Jack asked.

"Last Friday, and the number of the phone coincides with a number on Raheem's phone that he called several times. "

"Then we have a connection. A call went from Raheem to Matteem and Matteem to Mr. X and Karem to Mr. X. And we know that Mr. X is somewhere in a remote section of Maryland. Well, everybody's gotta be some someplace. The job is finding out where."

"Everybody's gotta be some place. Wow! That's profound. You got the makings of a philosopher." Nicole said as her small, trying to control herself, tight smile gave way to a laugh."

"I think we could better use a magician then a philosopher." Rachel's practical nature came through.

"We don't have much," Todd said, "just a remote area of Maryland. The person who received the messages could be long gone and what does it have to do with finding Matteem?"

Jack decided against his second bagel. "This is where you have to," Jack substituted a second coffee, "put your self in the mind of a terrorist. First you consider the situation he's in. Matteem's two big plans failed. His attacks on us failed and he lost his cell members. In addition to that we have found some of his safe houses. Now, if we think about this, I think we will all come up with the sane answer."

Nicole spoke first, "Everybody's gotta be someplace, but I think Matteem would want to change that place."

The others all gave signs of affirmation. Jack said, "I think he would be looking for a very secure place with comforting conspirators around him. The receiving end of those calls may be the answer. Todd, let's all go in and you can bring up Google Earth."

The group arranged their chairs around Todd's computer. Rachel said, "Why do I have the feeling I'm at Game Works?"

"It could be all the signs and colorful posters," Nicole suggested.

"Do you like it?" Todd asked. "I think it's cool."

"I think it's wonderful." Jack said tongue in cheek as the earth expanded in front of him and settled on a close up of the Maryland coast. "Zoom in on the Patuxent River area."

Todd clicked the plus sign, scrolled over to the area where the Patuxent River meets the Chesapeake Bay and then slowly scrolled north. "I don't know about you guys but this makes me feel like smashing a few crabs."

"That does sound good but oh so messy," Nicole said.

"Two of the communications seemed to come from out on the river and one from Route 5. I think most of that area is farm country. Some of the towns are no more that four corners." Jack pointed to the screen. "Follow five down."

"It is, "Rachel said, "It's very remote. I remember it as being mostly Mennonite country. I went to the Patuxent River Naval Air station a couple times."

"If Matteem has joined up with a cell down there," Jack said, "the cell would stand out. They all know each other. I don't think it would be hard to find a group of strangers. The hard part will be to interview locals. It's spread out and they might be suspicious of us."

"We need a good ruse and I don't think a bag lady would work," Rachel said.

"I think we can come up with something, but first we'll check with the post office on the residents listed in this ten mile area on the south side of the Putuxent River. That should cover the area that the communication came from." Jack pointed to this section on the map. "Todd you work with the Post Office on this and get a Geological Survey map of the area. If there is a cell operating in the area, they are probably renting or leasing a place. Contact the realtors in the area and find out about rental property."

They all went their separate ways for lunch and when Jack returned and stepped out of the chute he heard a thud noise followed by an other and then another. He walked toward the exercise room and when he got there Nicole threw a knife at a target at the end of the room. The knife landed a ring away from a bull's eye. Jack joined Frank and Rachel in their, "Well done. Good shot. Nice throw," exclamations.

Jack said, "What's next sword fighting?"

"Hey, don't knock it. It was very effective Tuesday," Rachel said.

"True, true, I take it back," Jack raised his open palms in front of him. "Anything that works."

"And," Nicole said, "no calories."

Frank didn't, say anything, he just stood there with the look of a proud mentor.

When Todd joined them, he had lunch at his computer, they went on with their meeting, and he said, "I found one interesting situation. There is a building near the water that's leased by a Sportsman's Club and they are a group of people from the D. C. area."

"Maybe we could go down and look into joining the club. I could use some fishing right now," Jack said.

"No, that won't work. I asked the realtor, who also thought that would be a good idea because there are no other clubs in the area, and he said it was a private club with membership by invitation only."

"It's just what we're looking for— an exclusive club. Albeit they aren't good sports. Tomorrow we'll spend a day in the country. Make the preparations and arrangements you have to make, as for today I think we should all meet at the Crab Mallet later for dinner. I haven't stopped thinking about smashing a few crabs since you mentioned it Todd."

Chapter 40

Smash Bang

The large ship's helm with its carved, gold, inlayed lettering, signifying this to be the "Crab Mallet", hung over the entry way to the restaurant. Two large oak doors fitted with wrought iron hinges and handles accessed the restaurant.

Once inside, various fishing traps, lines, nets and buoys hung from the rough hewn timbers used for the rafters that ran the length of the room. The planked walls with the portholes added to the impression that one was inside of a nineteenth century sailing ship.

The team collected at a round, wooden table at the far corner of the restaurant. An old ship's lantern hung over the table. They stood and waited while a waitress wearing black pants, blue and white shirt, and a Greek fishing hat, spread Kraft paper from a roll over the table. After everyone was seated she passed out menus and crab mallets.

"This place is neat. I never new it was here." Todd said while he tried the mallet on the table.

"That's because it wasn't opened until about six months ago. I usually have crabs when I go down to the shore, but when you mentioned crabs; I remembered this place," Jack hefted his mallet, "nothing like fresh crabs and beer."

"Where do you go when you go to the shore?" Nicole asked

"Ocean City." Jack said and thought —I'd love to take you there.

"I love that area," Rachel said, "my husband and I camp at Assateague State Park. That's the Barrier Island—it's a National Seashore."

"It must be hard on you and your husband when you have to be away and it's not the safest job in the world." Nicole said.

"We're used to it. We were both in the service for quite awhile and we don't have children. That's where I met him."

"What's he doing now?"

"He's in charge of security at the University." Rachel turned to Jack. "That brings up a question, about tomorrow, will we be staying over?"

"There's always that possibility, so come prepared. That area is very remote and if we have to I'm not sure we will find rooms, so bring sleeping bags and camping supplies." Jack looked at Todd who was stuffing his large white napkin in the neck of his shirt to function as a bib. It was just in time too, the waitress brought over the crabs and the smashing began.

After satisfying their cravings, Rachel and Todd left. Jack and Nicole had both order another beer and it was placed in front of them. They both looked at each other with the same look of an unexpected reality. Nicole said, "They left early."

"They did. Does this mean we're on a date?"

"I think it does."

"You know my place is not far from here." After he said it, he had an awkward feeling.

"Jack, that still bothers me."

"What?"

"That you still live there. I don't think it's safe. I'm concerned about you."

Is that all, he thought, but said, "I actually installed some new security measures which are unique and one of them helped save my life in that attempted bombing. Would you like me to show them to you? One of them is bound to surprise you."

"Jack, is this a new version of 'Come up to my room and I'll show you my etchings". If it is you don't have to get that creative. I'd love to see your new security measures, but I don't think I'll feel very safe."

In front of his apartment door he pointed to the small circular area that would light up if the motion detectors had gone off in the room while he was away. Inside his apartment, Jack said, "If I'm inside, the alarm can then be changed to sound an alarm if there is an attempted entry at either the doors or windows."

"Oh, I'm impressed. I like the way you have it decorated, a little on the manly side, but well done."

"Would you like a glass of wine?"

"Sounds good."

"Look around while I get the wine."

Nicole walked into the bedroom and said. "It gives me chills to think what was under that bed."

Nicole joined Jack holding the wine in the living area. He handed her one and clinking his glass against her glass said. "Let's hope it's in the past."

They both sat on the couch and Nicole said. "You said something about a surprise."

"That I did and it's the biggest security measure in the apartment. Look around and see if you can discover it."

Nicole spoke as she looked around and described the apartment. "The first thing I saw when I came in was the entry way with the bookcase on the right and the coat closet on the left. Next was the living room in front of me with sliding doors to a patio. The kitchen with a breakfast bar led off to the right and the bedroom off to the left." Nicole stood up took a sip of her wine and slowly perused the room. Jack followed suite.

She gave another walk through of the apartment with him following and then stopped back in the living area. "Is it something I can see?"

"Actually this is a test to see if it can be noticed visually. It's possible it could be deducted but I don't think you can."

"Sometimes to deduct something you have to think about what you don't see and what I don't see is a computer or office which I know you must have."

"That's incredible; you're good, really good, in fact to me, it's as good as finding it." Jack went over picked up the wine and poured them a drink to celebrate.

Nicole was enjoying Jack's excitement but said, "But I didn't find anything."

"That's all right—you knew there was a missing room. In time you'd find it."

"Oh, OK. I think it would be a long time."

Jack went over to the bookcase. "How do you like my book collection?"

"Jack, are you going to read to me?"

"No, but look at this." His hand went to the side of the bookcase and when it came back, so did the bookcase.

Nicole was beyond surprise—shock would be a better description. The arched, detailed eyebrows lifted, the mouth opened and she made a quick inhalation. "It's the old haunted house. I don't believe it." She stepped into the hidden room.

" I told you, you were on to it. It's the second bedroom that I used for my computer room. I put a bed in here, made a bookcase door and now it's my safe room."

Nicole turned and closed the bookcase door. "With a bed—how convenient." She set down her glass of wine and repeated the move with his. "I don't know if you should feel safe though." She moved closer with raised arms and continued. "After crabs, beer, wine and all that sweet talk about security systems, I just might seduce you."

He reached out and took her up turned face in his hands and gave her a gentle kiss. Another one followed and then the longer one which begins the fusion process, with it his hands dropped and began to caress her shapely contour. This no longer was a safe room—it was heaven.

Nicole left early in the morning to go home and get ready for work. She lived with her mother in a Victorian home in the suburbs. It worked out well for both of them; she having had some failed relationships and her mother was a widow. She felt it was secure not having her name attached to the property and she always mention it as her apartment in conversation. She turned the corner to her street and chuckled. My God, what a night. Crabs, beer, wine, a hidden room—a broad smile revealed her happiness and humor—and oh yes, Jack. Especially Jack.

Chapter 41

It's Not an Old Tire

At the mouth of the Patuxent River two crab fishermen tugged on a trap line and found it to be snagged. This wasn't an uncommon event. They circled over the trap and dropped a grappling hook. With two lines attached, they began to haul it up. It was unusually heavy and they called to a third fisherman for help. At about three feet from the surface they saw a large white shape figure draped over the trap.

The first fisherman said, "What the hell is that?"

The second said, "There's a cinder block tied to it."

A gasp followed by, "Holy shit, it's a body," came from the third.

Securing the lines, they wrestled with the body to bring it on board. "The first man said, "Now what do we do?"

The second man looked toward the horizon. "Look, out there, there's a Coast Guard patrol boat."

Chapter 42

A Day in the Country

The van with the logo of Phantom Publishing Company professionally lettered on both sides pulled into a general store occupying one of the four corners. Jack was still enjoying his clever selection of the name because it was true, there was no such publishing company. The other corners were occupied by an old gas station now solely being used as a repair shop, a farm equipment business, and a fabric store. This was Buntville, thinking about this, Jack thought perhaps the name originated because of its being a very light hit in the world of villages.

After sharing this revelation with the rest of the group, he looked at his GPS and said. "This is the only business area close to that Sportsman's Club. Todd, you and I will go in under the ruse of doing a magazine article on the club and the area. We'll ask about the location of the club and try to get as much information about the members as we can. You can show an interest in their magazine and book section. These are rural people, so we must do this in a manner that is slow and indirect and arouses their curiosity."

The small bells, that hung over the door, announced their entrance. There was no visible human response, but the aroma of fresh ground coffee, cheese, and scented candles greeted them with tranquility. Bulk barrel containers holding beans, potatoes, pickles and other food supplies sat on the wide wood plank floor in the front of the store. The back of the store had metal bins that held nails and other hardware items. This back section had double doors that led to a dock area at the side of the building where trucks could pull up for loading. Jack saw two men retuning from there after helping a customer load his truck and one went back to the hardware section and one came to the checkout counter in the front of the store. He gave Jack a little nod and tight smile when he returned behind the counter.

Jack nodded back and mumbled, "Morin'," he then turned slowly to take in the whole store. "I think you got everything anyone would need."

"Hope so," the clerk replied.

"It's like a museum," Todd said.

Not knowing how this would be taken Jack said, "Todd why don't you go over and see what kind of magazines and books they sell. See if there are any on the area. Taking the hint he went over to the section that had a sundry of items that you would find in any Mom and Pop store.

This gave Jack the opportunity to explain their business for being in the area. He took a few steps closer to a rack holding fishing equipment that was also closer to the counter and said. "We're from Phantom Publishing and we're doing an article on the area."

"It'll probably be a real short article," the clerk said followed up with a smug look.

"Well," Jack turned back to the fishing rack and then back to the clerk, "it's a great fishing area and you must have a lot of sports clubs around here."

"People around here aren't into clubs, although there is one— private though—city folks."

Jack moved to the counter where he saw a clear plastic display covering a large wheel of cheese. "Boy that looks good. Is that extra sharp cheddar?"

"Yup, get it from the Mennonites. They make good cheese. It's aged a long time. Would you like a sample?"

"Would I? Thank you. When I was a boy we called that rat's cheese."

"I still do." The clerk's eyes had actually twinkled.

The ice had been broken. "Todd, come over here and try this cheese."

The clerk cut off a couple of wedges and said. "Let me get you some crackers with that."

Todd reacted to the tasting with, "Sweet man, that's awesome."

At this, the clerk looked a little bewildered.

"That's the best I've had for a long time. It really grabs you." And then thinking of the two in the van he said, "I'll take a pound of that, a box of crackers and some sodas. Maybe there is material for an article here and I don't think we could do one with out including your store. What do you think, Todd?"

"Absolutely, this is where it's at man, this is the place."

The clerk beamed and called out to the man in the back, "David, I want you to meet somebody." He faced Jack and said, "My name is Cliff."

"Mine's Jack and this is Todd." Jack withdrew a map from his pocket and asked. "That sports club could be included in the article too. Could you show me the location on here?"

The clerk bent over the map, pointed and said. "It's about four miles down River Road. When you get to Old Mill Road you take a left and it's on the right."

"Having a lot of sportsmen around must be good for your business."

"It helps."

"It must help on your beer sales." Jack laughed.

"No, they never buy beer, just groceries."

"Is there a camp site in the area, if we decide to stay over and try some fishing?"

David answered, "There's one at the end of River, Rene's Campground. I t has a dock, a loading ramp, tent spaces and small trailer spaces."

Cliff added, "And you can rent small boats there."

"Well, thanks for everything. We'll come back when where putting this together."

Jack had Rachel pull over further down the road when he thought he was out of view of the store. "It's time for a special snack."

Todd past out the cheese, crackers and soda. Nicole accepted the snacks and said. "How did it go in there?"

Before Jack could answer, Todd enthusiastically gave them a summary. "But the thing was they were very offish at first, and then Jack with timing and some sweet talk had them in the palm of his hand."

"Sweet talk? Was it about security systems?" Nicole teased.

"Security systems? No, about cheese and including them in an article about the area. But Jack," Todd said, "I got a sense that the remark about the beer sales was important."

"I think I can answer that. The people we're looking for don't use alcohol, right Jack," Rachel said.

"Right and he mentioned that they bought groceries but not any fishing supplies. I think we got some good information from them."

"I like them, after you break the ice, they seem all right."

"They're just regular down to earth people. I feel a little guilty about using the "writing an article" ruse." Jack said in a somber tone.

"I think I can take care of that," Todd said, "I have a friend who writes articles about places like that for the Sunday magazine. I'll tell him—he'll be glad to get the tip."

"OK, Rachel, let's take a ride down River Road and check out the facilities and then we will check out the club that Matteem may be using for cover."

Chapter 43

Squawking Gulls

The team drove around Rene's Campground and found it to be wooded, very clean, and the wash room facilities looked new. It appeared to be about half occupied and that was just a guess because the spaces were large and laid out in such a way that afforded privacy. This surprised Jack because he expected, given this was such a remote area, it to be more primitive and perhaps not as well cared for. There was a mix of campers some with small RVs, others tents. Most of the tents were family size and had screen houses.

He pointed and said to Rachel, "Pull into #14 and we'll check it out."

The team splayed out from the van to view the area. Todd said, "Look you can see the water from here. "This is going to feel like a vacation."

"It's a good spot," Jack said, "let's see if it's available."

A boat was being launched from the ramp and several rental boats were tied to the dock. An office sign hung from a door attached to a building that looked like an addition to a home that was built in the thirties. Todd and Rachel walked down to the dock where squawking sea gulls made passes over an incoming fishing boat. Jack and Nicole went into the office and rang a bell on the counter with a sign requesting that they do so if they wanted service.

"I'll be with you in a minute," came from a back room. In a minute a middle age woman pushed a two wheeler, with an assortment of drinks on it, up to a large, colorful, old cooler with the "Coco Cola" logo on it.

"Now what can I do for you?" Was asked by a small, angular woman, who wiped her hands on her apron, as she moved behind the counter.

"We'd be interested in renting space #14 for the night, if it's available."

"Let me look. Yes, it's available. What do you have?"

This caught Jack off guard. "Have? Oh, yes, we have one van and one tent."

"Do you need an electrical hook up? Fourteen has one and its two dollars extra a night. Extra expense if you don't need one."

'That's fine. You have a very clean, attractive campground with all the conveniences."

Nicole said. "All the washrooms look new and I spotted a laundry."

"They are—and you did. We try to keep it up to date. Young people today aren't into roughing it so much. One couple asked if we had internet access. My husband told them he didn't even know where the internet was let alone have access to it. My husband is quite humorous." A proud smile spread over, what they assumed to be, Mrs. Rene's face.

Jack nodded his head in the direction of the ramp. "I see you have boat rentals and is that a public boat ramp?"

"Oh no, that's private. We charge a launching fee."

"We made a wrong turn and passed a Sportsman's Club on the way here. We were thinking about checking it out. Do they use your facilities too?" After he said this, Jack wasn't sure if the question was too direct.

"No. I don't know what kind of sportsmen they are, but I don't think they're fishermen. Never seen them around here." Mrs. Rene turned the register around so Jack could fill it in and sign it.

It was decided by the team that Jack and Todd would use the van and Rachel and Nicole would use the tent. Rachel said she loved tenting and had brought her own tent which she set up with the speed and efficiency of one having a lot of camping experience. Jack of course would have like to suggest the other possibility of Rachel and Todd in the tent and he and Nicole in the van but knew this was just a fantasy.

Jack called the team to the picnic table for a planning session. "What do we have? We have sportsmen who don't buy any fishing supplies at the local country store and don't use any of the facilities at Rene's and I think, being a country person who would likely know everybody in the area, she would have mentioned something about them."

"Maybe they're hunters," Nicole said.

"Or maybe they just use it for target practice and training," Rachel added.

"Those are the things we're going to have to find out. It's getting late in the afternoon and I think the locals might get suspicious of strangers moving about at night. Let's go see if there interested in buying advertising in our directory of the area."

They would never find out. Before they even had a chance to get to the two and a half storied building they saw an assortment of signs—No Trespassing, Private Property, No Solicitation.

Chapter 44

We Could be Wrong

The next morning the van, with its logo removed, past the club and took the first right onto a dirt road. Todd dropped the three bird watchers off and returned to the camp site where he stood watch with the radio. The three bird watches in their camouflaged clothes and binoculars climb over a barbed wire fence. The sparse underbrush in this area made it easy to walk through. Jack cringed as he snapped twigs under his foot.

They continued to walk toward the direction of the club house. Nicole whispered, "Look, that's a pop up target."

"You may have hit the nail on the head, Rachel," Jack said, "There's a simulated building."

A thud and a groan came from Jack's left side—he turned to the sound. Nicole grabbed the red covered spot with her hand and dropped to her knees. Immediately he and Rachel were hit and both also dropped to the ground. Recognizing their color was green, Jack said in a low voice, "Hide your weapons."

The three of them stayed in their position and watched the five men surrounding them close in. Four of them stopped about fifteen feet away and the fifth came closer. The team rose and faced him.

"This is private property, you walked into our game. Didn't you see the signs, the fence?"

"Yes, we did, we climb it. We saw a Pileated Woodpecker and couldn't resist getting a little close for proper identification. He kept moving from tree to tree and without thinking about it we were drawn further onto the property. I do apologize."

"I do understand your enthusiasm, I enjoy watching them. I hope you can appreciate our enthusiasm for the game and I'm sorry about plastering you with paint."

At the campsite retelling the story to Todd, Jack added, "Paint ball, a paint ball club that explains everything. Not hunting or fishing, but paint ball, although it doesn't rule out your idea, Rachel, of a training camp. It was impossible to get any pictures for identification with them wearing helmets with shields and various camouflaged outfits. We could be following a wrong lead here, but we will stay on and do some surveillance on them. Nicole would you go up and asked Mrs. Rene to book us for a couple more nights."

Jack was sitting with Rachel, who was reading an adventure novel, at the picnic table, when Todd leaned out of the van and called to Jack. "It's Bill."

"I am not sure. We may be following a false lead but we going to take a course of surveillance on a group we found down here." Jack then went on to detail the encounter with the group.

"So, what you're telling me is that my special Disaster Aversion Team was taken out by a paint ball team. That's very encouraging." Bill laughed. Jack was embarrassed.

"I don't know how this will affect your plan, but Matteem has risen to the occasion."

"What! Where? How did they find him?"

"Some crab fisherman pulled him up with their trap near the mouth of the Patuxent and called the coast guard."

"How do they know it's Matteem?"

"The Coast Guard took the body to the morgue at the Patuxent Naval Air Station. They sent the information and pictures to all the local authorities for identification. They also sent the information to the secret headquarters of the National Counter Terrorism Center. They matched it up with Interpol's and Todd's pictures and information. One of the unique identifying marks was a cicatrix running from his face to his neck."

"How did he die?"

"This is where it gets real serious, Jack, when they made the identification, they called for an immediate autopsy. The results showed he died from nerve gas. And the only thing he was wearing at the time was a white lab coat."

"Nerve gas? What the hell are we dealing with Bill? I find it interesting that the location is not far down river from where we are. That turns our search for Matteem, in a safe house, to a search for a cell who considered him a liability. Did they find any identifying marks on the lab coat?"

"They didn't say."

"Todd will find out," Jack said.

"Good hunting, I hope you can find them before all hell breaks loose."

"Thanks, we're going to give it our best."

Jack click off and leaned out of the van, Nicole just returned from the Office, He waved to both of them to come in the van.

"I just talk to Bill and he told me some important developments. A body was found by crab fishermen and then collected by the Coast Guard. The body was identified as Matteem and the cause of death was nerve gas." Jack glance from one team member to the other and saw their expressions grow serious as they pondered on the cause of death.

"If he was in the water any length of time," Todd asked, "how did they identify him"

"The first thing they noticed was a cicatrix running from the side of his face down to his neck. If you look at the photos we have, the full face view is not as favorable as a side view, but it's there." Jack pulled out the photos from his bag.

"Say what man? Cicatrix?" Anything sounding like science fiction got Todd's attention.

"Yes, it's the technical term they use for a scar.

"You said he died of nerve gas," Nicole said, "that's really unusual isn't it?"

"It is, and it means they have access to it and, if that's the case, they are planning a catastrophic event. I think they made a big mistake in using it on Matteem. They show their hand. Bill felt the same way and said that this will put all the agencies on high alert. Another unusual thing is that he was only wearing a lab coat. Todd, follow that up and see if there were any identifying marks on it. You know; maybe some company or laundry marks. Meanwhile we will set a plan for scoping out the sports tomorrow. I'm especially curious about this group and now more so with the finding of Matteem's body nearby,"

Chapter 45

No Runs, No Hits

Acar the cell leader of the more military trained and experienced group covering as the Sportsman's Club sat in Dr. Ketchum office. Acar told him about the paint ball incident. "Their explanation could be true, but when I reviewed the surveillance tapes taken at the front gate of two people who approached yesterday, I thought it resembled two of the bird watchers." Acar laid the photos on the desk

Dr. Ketchum looked at the photos and activated his intercom. "Sanjay bring in the pictures you found in Matteem's briefcase."

Lining up the pictures in front of him Dr. Ketchum said. "They match." He then turned the pictures for Acar to view.

"They do." Acar picked up the two pictures from Matteem's briefcase. "They have names on them. Jack Dunn and Nicole Burns."

"It's too bad you used paint balls on them," Dr. Ketchum said.

"I agree."

"Probably even more so when I tell you that these are the people who took out Karem and Habid—two of your most skilled and experienced men."

Acar's face tightened and his normally deep set eyes narrowed and retreated even further. "Revenge will be very sweet."

"Not yet. We must not over react. We don't know if they found any connection with you and Matteem or they know about the lab."

"Matteem?"

"Yes, they are clever; they are trying to track his movements since he left Washington. Probably through those stupid, unnecessary calls he made. I don't think they have anything or they would have acted in a more direct manner. For now, limit your activity and don't come back here. I noticed you brought those racks of water bottle samples and compliment you on keeping your guard up."

Chapter 46

Beating the Bush

The next day the team executed their plan. With Todd driving and Jack in the front seat, they took a left on River, drove past Old Mill, and made a u-turn on River. When they were opposite the end of Old Mill and River, they dropped off Nicole and turned on to Old Mill Road. This provided the least amount of exposure for Nicole as she scrambled into the brush. At the north end of Old Mill, where it meets Sandy Point Road, they took a left, slow down until they found adequate bush and dropped off Rachel. The van returned to Rene's Campground where they waited for any information. Even though they had only one vehicle, Jack thought that any car leaving the club could be caught up with if they were given the direction the vehicle was going in.

The signal came from Nicole. "A dark SUV just left the club and turned north on Old Mill."

"Copy, we're on it." Todd pulled out of Rene's, moved quickly down River and made the right on Old Mill. Jack was satisfied when he looked for Nicole and she was nowhere to be seen.

"They coming your way, Rachel," Jack said.

"I heard," she answered, "they're not in view yet."

"It's starting to rain. That's good," Jack said.

"Why's that?" Todd asked.

"People are not as observant when it's raining. Though, not good for Nicole or Rachel."

"They just pulled up to the stop sign and are turning right. You must have them in view. I can see your van." Rachel turned up her collar and snapped up her camouflaged jacket.

Todd turned right and at about a mile down the road the SUV turned left into Ketchum's Chemical Testing Company. By the time they were abreast of the entrance, a man carrying two wire racks of bottles got out of his SUV. Todd went further down the road and made a U-turn at a safe viewing distance from the company.

"Look, he's coming out now." Jack looked at his watch. "I would think you could drop off water samples faster than that."

"He was probably just blogging with the receptionist," Todd said, then added, "What do we do now?"

"Blogging? Yes, or maybe he had to use the men's room. We'll pick up Nicole and Rachel—who must be soaked by now—and return to Rene's. While they dry off and clean up, we'll find out all we can about the chemical company."

Todd opened the custom made cabinet in the wall of the van that held his computer, lowered the door which double as a table top and secured it to two brackets. "Look, I got a message back on the lab coat," Todd said, "Do you want to check it out now?"

"Why not?"

Todd read it aloud, "They're no identifying marks on the laboratory coat." He gave an internal sigh and added. "That's not going to help us."

"On the contrary, most hospitals, laboratories, or any organization that used lab coats would have a logo, name, or laundry mark on them. That in it self is unusual and may help us in identifying where it came from.”

Todd manipulated his fingers through all the normal search engines looking for information on the KCTC, as he began calling it, and printed out the information which Jack perused.

Jack activated his V5, the name now being used by the team for the Vault COMM 5, and heard the reply. “Bill here.”

“We followed a sportsman to Ketchum’s Chemical Testing Company. All the information we are reviewing shows it to be a legitimate company. He carried two racks that appeared to be some kind of samples with him.”

“I’ll have it checked out deeper. Is there any way you can check it out on a more personal level?”

“I thought about that and have come up with a plan, but I’ll need your help. While we were scoping it out, the only other vehicle to drive in was a UPS truck. If it could be arranged for Rachel to pose as a driver, or maybe a trainee, we could get access to the building.”

After a pause and some clicking Bill said, “There’s a distribution point twenty miles from you. I’ll get back to you after making the arrangements. They might only delivery once a day, so the earliest would be tomorrow. I’ll get back to you.”

“I think we’ll be spending the night in the rain.”

The four huddled in the van playing cards. During the game Jack brought them up to date on the plan. He looked out of the van window and added, “Do you guy’s want to switch around, you might be more comfortable in here.”

“My tent has never leaked,” Rachel said.

“I think we can handle some bad weather,” Nicole said.

Their tone suggested to Jack that he may have uncommonly crossed the chauvinistic line. Not being able to recall a question that expressed his true but outdated concern, he changed the subject. "Three jacks. Rachel, tomorrow you'll take on the role as a UPS trainee. They will be making a delivery, in fact we have learned that they make regular deliveries to KCTC, which is a point added for their legitimacy, and this will get us access to the inside.

"The manager of UPS is the only one in on this and you'll meet him at 6:30 am at their depot twenty miles from here. He'll have a uniform for you and will introduce you to the regular driver."

"Three aces." It was Nicole's turn to change the subject.

Jack folded and then continued, "What camera did you bring?"

Rachel reached into her bag and took out a baseball cap. "This is very clever. It has the save the Rain Forrest logo on it. If you look close, you'll see the lens is cleverly hidden in the monkey's eye. I like it better than the belt camera because you can get a higher perspective and you control it with this." She reached back in her bag and pull out a remote. "This is small enough to be concealed in your hand, or be held and activated from your pocket."

"Excellent, but does the UPS uniform include a hat? Let's find out." Jack called the manager and asked if it did. He was told it did. Jack said she would like to use her own and the manager asked Jack what the color was. Jack picked up the cap and described it to the manger as a brown cap with save the Rain Forrest logo on it. The manager said the color was perfect and he didn't think anyone would notice the logo was different.

It was Todd's turn to change the subject. "Full house." He drew in the pot.

"That hurts. Let's call it a night. We have to leave early to get there on time."

Chapter 47

Going Brown

"How long have you been with them, Rick?" Rachel asked.

"Eight years. If I heard the boss right, he said you would just be along for the morning run and I was to drop you off at the four corners Country Store in Buntville. Doesn't seem like much training."

"They're sending me to different routes to get familiarized with them. I am going to start as a substitute."

"Nice hat, are you one of those tree huggers?" Rick looked askance.

"Not in the extreme, but it's not a bad idea to conserve what we can."

"That's true." Rick swung the van into their first stop and with the speed and agility of a half back, handed her the clipboard, lifted the cargo door, pulled out the two wheeler, loaded the packages, and made the delivery. Rachel did the paper work.

On the next three deliveries the role was reversed. On the last of these three deliveries, she rolled the two wheeler through the front door of KCTC.

The man at the front desk said to Rick. "The job getting too much for you?"

"Trainee," Rick said.

"Where do you want these?" Rachel asked.

The man lifted the counter top and pointed. "In the storage room at the back."

"Getin' too lazy to do that, Turk?" Rick smiled at his retort.

Rachel managed to get a few shots on the way to the storage room and back, but she wanted more without the two wheeler inhibiting her. She had past the restroom and she also saw a stairwell leading to a lower level. She positioned the two wheeler and said. "Mind if I use the restroom?"

Later, after picking up Rachel at the Country Store, Todd plugged the memory stick into his computer. "Did anything strike you as unusual in there?" Jack said to Rachel, and then after he noticed the receptionist on the screen as being male. "Todd, he doesn't look like someone you would want to blog with, does he?"

"Man, you never know."

"That brings up an interesting point," Rachel said, "I didn't notice anything unusual, as you can see from the pictures, but now that I think of it , I didn't see any women working in there. Todd, go back to the lab area pictures. There weren't any women in the front area and look; I don't see any women working in there either."

"Good point. And you will notice that the employees are wearing lab coats. We'll take what we have learned back to the dorm for closer scrutiny. It doesn't seem like much, a paint ball club, an innocent looking lab, and finding out Matteem was killed by nerve gas, but maybe we'll find some small clue that will set the trail again. Matteem having been killed by nerve gas is a frightening piece of information. It is hard for a healthy mind to imagine how they're going to use it and worst yet, where are they?"

Chapter 48

Spotted

Acar came out of the country store and got in his car, turned the ignition key and hesitated before backing out. The UPS van stopped in front of the store and a woman jump out. Acar recognized her as one of the bird watchers. He shut off the engine and watched as the UPS van pulled away and the woman walked to the end of the parking lot. In a few moments, a white van pulled up and she got in the passenger side.

He quickly restarted the engine and pulled away and followed the white van at a safe distance down River Road. At the cross road with Old Mill Road, he turned left. The only place at the end of River Road was Rene's Campground, but if he continued following them the risk of being spotted would be increased, so after turning on Old Mill Road, he made a U-turn in front of the Sportsman's Club and went back on River Road. As he passed Rene's, he got a glimpse of the white van and the passengers getting out. There was no question about it now—he drove straight to Dr. Ketchum.

"We had a woman UPS employee here today," Dr. Ketchum said. "I was curious and asked Sanjay if she was a new driver. He said Turk told him she was in training. They're here to check us out. Too close for comfort."

Like a shark smelling blood, Acar said, "They're staying at Rene's. I could take them out tonight, remove everything from the campground and dispose of their bodies like we did Matteem's. Nobody would know the difference. They would think because of the weather they just packed up and left."

"Don't underestimate your enemy, Acar." Dr. Ketchum said in a stern tone. These people have already proven they're a formidable enemy. I wouldn't think I'd have to remind you."

This stinging remark flushed Acar's face and changed his bravado demeanor. His chest expanded and contracted with in a long, slow rhythm in an attempt to control his hatred of these infidels.

Chapter 49

Here a Rabbit, There a Rabbit

At the table in Jack's office, each member of the team reviewed the history of evidence on the terrorist prior to their planning session. The interrogations of the three home grown bomb carriers did not provide any important information. This didn't surprise Jack it was to be expected. Their knowledge of the operation, or of the chain of command, would be limited to insure security, but following the source of their recruitment the interrogators might gain information that would help to prevent the spread of hatred. Jack set this report down and pick up the forensic photos of Karem and Habid, the two assassins killed in their assassination attempt at the bomb factory.

Jack got up, went to his desk and returned to the table with a magnifying glass in hand. After looking at the photo, he turned to Todd, who was sitting next to him and said, "Here take this and look at his boot. Do you see anything?"

"It's a green mark on a brown boot."

"Todd, check with the forensic people and see exactly what that is." Jack handed the photo to Nicole who in return handed it to Rachel.

Jack picked up the photos that Rachel had taken in the KCTC. "Well done Rachel, you covered the whole area."

"A trip to the restroom helped and after that I saw a back stairway leading down to a lower level. Those are the

pictures you're looking at now. As you can see it turned
out to be just a normal office supply room."

"Rachel, do you have the disc?"

"Yes."

"Put it in the computer so we can get a larger
view."

Jack clicked slowly through the pictures, stopped
and back up one picture. "That's a cage with a rabbit in it.
Rachel, do you know whose office that is?"

"That's Dr. Ketchum's."

Jack proceeded with the scanning. He stopped
when he came to the testing laboratory. "Look, there on
the counter against the back wall, another rabbit."

Todd returned and took his place at the table. "Did
I hear rabbit? Cool man, I used to have a rabbit. He was
all black I called him Darth Vader."

"Jack, "Nicole said, "I think those rabbits triggered
something in your mind."

"It did, the Army used rabbits at their storage
facilities to test for leaking chemical warfare agents,
although I don't see any need for that in there."

"It's probably that one of the employees ended up
with too many rabbits." Todd reasoned.

"I'll show you what we looking at while you were
gone, Todd." Jack started the scanning with the first
pictures of the front reception area.

Nicole this time reacted with a quick turn to Jack's
face and then to the screen and repeated the motion. She
said, "Ill bet there are a lot of scientific books in that
bookcase. Didn't you tell me you built a bookcase, Jack?"

Jack stared at the bookcase. He immediately
recognized the innuendo. "Yes, I did. It would be
interesting if it was from the same plan." After giving
Todd a chance to view the rest of the pictures, Jack asked,
"Todd did you get any information on the mark?"

"They sent this report," Todd answered.

Jack took the report and read it. Then he said, "It's a water soluble green pigment dye. Todd, ask them if it is the type used in the manufacture of paint balls."

"Wouldn't that be something if it linked Karem and Habid to the Sportsman's Club," Rachel said.

"It would be a big break," Jack said, and also thought, it would also be a big break if that bookcase led to a lower level concealing a chemical laboratory handling chemical weapons. Let's take a break while Todd finds out.

Todd returned, picked up a soda and sat at the table. "Affirmative, that's the answer. They can't say that this stain came from a paint ball, but this is the material that they use in making them."

"I think we covered everything we have," Jack said, "but before I begin to summarize it, Rachel I have a question for you, how large was that lower level?"

"Oh, about 12 by 24 feet."

"That would be only about a third of the size of the upper level. That presents another possibility that there is a large area on that lower level that we haven't seen."

"Are you thinking that this could be an area where they produce nerve gas? When I've seen pictures of these types of facilities they are always large compounds," Todd said.

"You're right, Todd, it would be too small for a chemical factory, but not too small for storage and transferring it to some type of delivery system and this could be a place for experimenting with delivery systems. It would have to have some very sophisticated equipment and run by some very qualified scientists."

"What about Dr. Ketchum's background?" Nicole asked, "Is there anything that shows he's capable of carrying out this type of project?"

"No, there's no history of him having this type of experience. That doesn't tell us much though, he could be self taught and there could be other scientists working with him that we haven't found out about.

"Now we will proceed with the facts and theories so far. Matteem was taken out because he was a great risk to a big plan in process. It back fired with the finding of his body. The fact he was murdered indicates they were in fear of him, because of his dealings with us, exposing their plan. The way it was done was a big mistake. It reveals they are in procession of nerve gas. It would also indicate they have a chemical facility for handling nerve gas. Putting everything together, A chemical company close to the area where Matteem's body was found, the cell phone activity to this area from other terrorists, the green mark that could connect Karem and Habrid to the Sportsman's Club, and two rabbits at the KCTC—Jack did not mention the possibility of a bookcase hiding a room to the lower level—I think we're going to do some covert activity at the KCTC and Sportsman's Club."

Chapter 50

Down Stream

They had to wait three days to get the least amount of moonlight and avoid the weekend when they thought the Sportsman's Club was used the most. Todd was everywhere on the Coast Guard Utility Boat Big (UTL) checking out the electronic equipment and Lt. Harrison even showed him the engine. This was going on while the boat sliced through the water heading east to the KCTC dock on the Patuxent River. The other team members sat facing each other on benches that ran along the sides of the cabin.

Finishing his tour, Todd joined the others and sat down next to Jack. He looked, Jack thought, with his black watch cap and camouflaged face like he had been doing this for years. Todd had become very enthusiastic about his role as a team member and had even changed his spike hair style and toned down his wardrobe, but he was still Todd and Jack was glad of that. Jack worried about Todd because he did not have the experience or training the others had. In the other operations his part as a team member was always a step out of harm's way. But this time there was no way to avoid it.

To scope out both places, pick up the physical evidence they needed for DNA analysis or other clues as to the terrorists objectives, and to provide a back up for each member, he split the team into two groups. Todd would be Rachel's backup.

Todd turned in his seat and lean out to view the shore line. In doing so he bumped Jack. Jack looked down at the hard object that bumped him, he said. "What's that? You're carrying?" In this operation, Todd's role would be as a back up for Rachel by acting as a look out and to inform the others if there was trouble.

"Yeah, it's a 9mm Glock."

"You know how to use that?" Jack asked.

"Oh sure, Frank's been training me." The proud expression that crossed Todd's face was one that you would expect after seeing somebody that visited the Pope.

It seems that Frank had taken over the responsibility for training the team, Jack thought, and the only reply he could come up with was, "Good, but be careful."

Rachel said, "He's pretty good with it too."

Jack thought but didn't say, I hope so, he's your backup.

Lt. Harrison shut off the running lights, told the helmsman to cut back on the engine and then told the team to stand by. Jack told the team to put on their goggles and check their maps. The debarking went smoothly and the team move quickly for the cover of the brush at the shore line.

The team moved through the brush parallel to Sandy Point Road in the direction of the KCTC. Jack stopped the team when they were in sight of the KCTC. Then addressing Rachel and Todd, said, "Refer to your GPS if you have problems, but it should be a straight run across Sandy and then you will cross the dirt road and trail we used before. This should bring you to the back of the club. Signal when you are there and ready to move in. We'll move at the same time."

Chapter 51

Where Oh Where is My MP5K?

Rachel and Todd did not encounter anything but woodland all the way to the dirt road and this brought them out in the area they had been when 'bird watching'. When they started through this area, she cautioned Todd about the pop up targets in the area. Rachel raised her hand to alert Todd when she saw the back of the Sportsman's Club. She slow done their pace and stopped at the edge of the woods and the beginning of the clearing that extended to the building.

"You stay here while I circle the building and look for any activity." Todd was very impressed with the way she moved through the brush and the fact that after she was about ten feet away he never saw her again until she scared him to death with, "I'm back. It looks like there's nobody home."

Todd noticed she was carrying some small sticks in her hand. "You goin' to start a fire?"

"No, I noticed the building has motion detector lights around the building. We're going to use these to check them out."

When they were about ten feet from the building, Rachel pointed to one of the detectors. Todd asked, "How can you tell they're not cameras?"

"The shape, they're bigger so they can hold bulbs, cameras have a small lens." Rachel handed Todd some of the sticks." She tossed her sticks in the area covered by the light.

"No light," Todd said.

"Right, but that could be because the bulb is burned out. Let's try the next one." This time Todd tossed the sticks—no light.

"Now, to find an entry." Rachel moved in close to the building and followed the foundation until she came to a casement window.

They both dropped to the ground. "Do you think they have a security system?" Todd asked.

"We know of the camera on the front gate and the motion detector lights. My guess would be that the front and back doors would have adequate locks, but it not unusually to have all this and nothing on the basement windows." Sliding her gear bag off her shoulder, she took out a glass cutter, tape and a small hammer.

Looking in her bag, Todd was surprise to see all of Rachel's tools. He said, "You've got everything in there. I think you could get into Fort Knox."

"It's my bag of tricks." She made the cut, taped the area and tapped it with the hammer. Removing the glass gave her enough room to reach in, turn the lever handle and push the window open. With her flashlight in hand she leaned in and checked out the area below the window. "It's a clear drop to the floor."

A perplexed Todd said, "I'm going to get through there?"

Taking off her jacket, she handed it to Todd with her gear bag. "Hand me these when I'm in along with yours. Lay on your stomach and back in feet first. I'll grab your legs when you're in."

In the cellar Rachel's flashlight picked up the electrical box on the wall. They moved some boxes and an old ladder backed chair to get to it and in the process Todd had to stifle a sneeze brought on by the dust. Rachel opened the box and said, "There's no new wiring, or any new circuits. I don't think they have any sophisticated system here." She pulled the main breaker. "I think we will be safer working in the dark."

"So far, so cool," Todd said.

"There's just one thing bothering me."

"What's that?"

"If they have an outside motion detector light system, why is it turned off?"

"Maybe it's turned off when nobody is here," Todd said.

"Maybe, or maybe they have abandoned the place and left somebody to watch, like at the bomb factory." Rachel watched Todd's face drop and get tense.

Rachel replaced her flashlight and Todd's with head sets from her gear bag. She said, "This will keep our hands free for picking up evidence. Take this; you'll need it for holding what you find." She handed him a canvas bag with shoulder straps. Next she took out digital camera and snapped it in her belt holder.

Pointing to the weapon in her bag, Todd said, "Is that what you use?"

"I use different weapons for different situations. That's a MP5K."

"Frank showed me the MP5."

"The difference is The MP5K is about half the length of the MP5. It's also 9mm, holds 19 rounds and has the automatic or burst options. The big advantage is its small size.

Rachel moved to the cellar staircase. "We're going to work our way through the building from bottom to top to see if anyone's home. When we reach the top floor we will search each room back down to the lower level. Let's stay close and work in adjacent rooms.

All the rooms in the building were sparsely furnished with old furniture. Aesthetically speaking, for the air hung damp and thick, there was no warmth to be found. It was barrack like in its coldness. The only things that gave it some connection to the past were the paintings and photos that hung on the wall. These items were paintings of pastoral scenes and pictures of game and fish that broke records. Probably these were left over from a time when it was used as a legitimate Sportsman's Club. Having seen no sign of life in their walk through, they started their room to room search for evidence on the top floor.

The staircase split the upper floor into three bedrooms and a bathroom on each side. Rachel and Todd took the one to their left. There was a window at the end of the hallway and two bedrooms on the left side and a bathroom and bedroom on the right.

The man in the attic couldn't use the ladder lying next to the attic trap door. It would make too much noise putting it down to the floor below. He would have to lower himself with his arms until he was as close to the floor as he could get, thereby minimizing the noise.

Dr. Ketchum's plan was to abandon the Sportsman's Club and the KCTC and to set up surveillance to determine if the agents were on to them. If they were, it would be a good time to slow them down by reducing their numbers.

The man standing watch now had cleverly removed a piece of lattice on four sides of the cupola on top of the building. Using this open space he could view the perimeter around the building. He also connected a listening device to the air duct that ran through out the building. He spent most of the time listening and making the rounds of the building. It was a stroke of luck when he saw them at the edge of the clearing, after that he followed their movements by sound. Following instructions to notify the Dr. of anyone's presents before he took action, he slung his Micro Uzi over his neck and lowered the trap door.

Rachel heard the squeak of the trap door and the thump that followed. She reached for the MP5K that should have been clipped on her belt, but wasn't. She swung her gear bag off her shoulder, unzipped it and grabbed her weapon. It was too late. He was standing in the doorway with his Uzi aimed. She swung her MP5K in position. It was an act of futility. He had the drop on her.

It didn't matter. The force of the round from the Glock threw the man forward and a burst from his Micro Uzi shattered the bathroom mirror. When he landed on the floor, Rachel could see Todd standing in the doorway across the hall. Todd still had his hands extended in a firing stance and a static expression on his face.

Rachel checked the man on the floor, removed his weapon and went to Todd. He slowly dropped his arms. Rachel said, "You save my life Todd, it's all right. You OK?"

"I don't know. It happened so fast. You wonder what you would do in a situation like that. He was going to kill you Rachel." Todd's eyes welled with emotion.

"You stopped him, you stopped him, Todd." She put her arms around him. "Let's call the boss and get out of here."

Chapter 52

Whoosh, Flash, Boom

Jack and Nicole reconnoitered the KCTC as soon as Jack got word that Rachel and Todd started theirs. Jack went clockwise and Nicole went counter clockwise around the building. When they met at the back of the building, Jack said, "I didn't see any entrance to the basement. Did you?"

"No, but I did see a large concrete area that could have been a bulkhead at one time."

"Not a common thing to do, unless your trying to conceal or contain something," Jack said.

"It also means that the only way to get into the basement is from the inside of the building. Didn't Rachel say that when she went down to a lower level she saw an office supply storage room? She didn't mention any door."

"No she didn't and it's logical to assume that the basement is much larger than that room and that the rest of the basement is being concealed. A possibility, which you silently signaled to me while watching the slide show, could be behind the bookcase. I wonder where you got that idea. Did you see any basement windows?"

"No."

"Neither did I." Jack started to move toward the building.

Nicole followed. "Have you decided on an entry?"

"This had a carriage house at one time. The carriage house is gone, but that long room at the back of the building was at one time used to enter the carriage house without going outside. We will have to go through two doors, but we can't be seen from the road and that will give us more time if we need it."

The first door was old and they were quick in getting through. The door to the main house had a newer lock system, but they didn't have any problem.

Inside the second door, Jack saw the stairwell to the lower level. He motion to Nicole in that direction and said, "Let's take a look at the supply room."

After checking the room for a door and not finding one, they return to the first floor and started their evidence gathering in the testing laboratory. Jack walked over to the empty rabbit cage. "The rabbit's gone," he said, "and this place looks like it has been cleaned out. Let's take a look at the other rooms."

The end of the hallway opened up to a large area with Dr. Ketchum's office on the right, the reception area, a low partioned office, and the bookcase against the wall. "Aha, the mysterious bookcase," Jack said.

"Shall we take a look?"

"Not yet, first we will take a look in the Dr.'s office and see if the other rabbit is there."

In the office Jack stood looking down at the empty rabbit cage. Nicole was standing next to the Dr's desk. She said, "Here's a good find."

"What's that?"

"An ash tray full of small cigars—perfect for DNA." Nicole picked the tray up with her gloved hands and emptied it into a plastic bag.

"Now we can check out the bookcase."

. Jack, although he didn't expect anything to move, stood in front of the bookcase and pulled. Nothing happened. He said, "Check on that side behind the bookcase and see if you find any opening mechanism. I'll check this side."

Jack reached behind the bookcase and ran his hand up and down the area. He felt nothing, then he ran it against the wall, bingo, a switch was on the wall. "I found it."

Nicole came and stood behind Jack. Jack reached in again and said, "Let's give it a try."

The bookcase slowly moved along the wall revealing an entrance to the lower laboratory. Jack moved to the revealed doorway.

Nicole, in an always watch your back habit, turned to scan the area. She said, "Wait, I see a lab coat on a coat rack in the Dr's office. I'll be right back."

Jack turned to face Nicole when she came back holding the lab coat. He said, "Let's see if it has any markings."

Nicole looked at the inside collar of the coat while Jack picked up the bottom. "I don't see anything," Nicole said, "do you?"

"No, but we have a case where the absence of markings is just as identifying."

The sound from the incendiary bomb came up the stairwell as a whoosh, followed by a blinding flash of light, then the boom. The fact Jack had his back to the opening and he shielded Nicole prevented them both from getting serious skin burns. The blast tumbled them to the floor. Jack felt the heat on the floor and the room filled with billowing, acrid smoke. Keeping a low profile they headed for the entrance they came in. They didn't make it. The smoke now filled the hallway and flames were breaking through the floor.

Jack said, "Get down—we'll go in the laboratory."

They crawled into the laboratory and stopped next to a window. Jack stood up, grabbed a metal lab stool and smashed the window. Outside they coughed and stumbled their way back to the knoll where the team separated.

Rachel and Todd were waiting for them. Jack managed to control his coughing long enough to say, "Call the Lieutenant and tell him we are on our way out."

The pickup went smoothly and once the boat was away from the shore and headed up stream the Lieutenant turned to observe the team. He said, "What the hell happen to you?"

Jack answered, "We walked into a trap. A lab coat saved us."

"A lab coat?"

"Yeah, we stopped to look at a lab coat after triggering a timing device that would have ignited a bomb to go off at a time when we would have been standing next to it."

A perplexed Lieutenant said, "Do these things happen to you very often?"

"Sometimes." He's impressed and he only knows half the story. He turned to Rachel and Todd. "How are you guys doing? Any injuries?"

They both responded with OK and fine.

The Lieutenant moved closer to Jack and Nicole after hearing their coughing spells. "I think you need some medical attention." He looked back at the shore line. "Look, you can still see the fire."

The rest of the trip went in silence.

Chapter 53

Grease Paint

How's everybody doing? Bill asked.

Jack took the seat in front of Bill's desk. "Fine, Nicole and I suffered smoke inhalation and Todd has been counseling with Cheryl. He was surprised by her credentials and he said that she being one of us made it easy for him to talk to her."

"You don't find too many receptionists with her qualifications. Cheryl has a doctor's degree in psychology and a lot experience in a few of the Intelligence Agencies. She also was a fitness trainer and offered her services in that field. Like you Jack, Frank and Cheryl volunteered, although they were in retirement.

"I don't know in my case if it was so much as volunteering. It was more that I was drawn in to save my ass."

"Whatever, I'm glad you signed on. This is quite a setback. Everything led us to their door and it was slammed in our face, or should I say blown up. When the collection crew got to the Sportsman's Club it was in ashes." Bill slid some pictures over to Jack. "This is what remains of both places. How do you think they found out you were on to them?"

"I'm not sure exactly, but I think when they confronted us at the Sportsman's Club, they became suspicious. Now, if they recognized Rachel at the KCTC and put both things together, they set up a trap to verify it.

They must have been quite sure though, because the KCTC was completely cleaned out." Jack picked up the pictures.

"It's one thing to try to find these bastards, but when you know they have access to nerve gas, time is the important factor in finding them." Bill pushed back in his chair and asked the tough questions. "So there it is. We know who, what there going to use, but where and when? What's your next move?"

"I'm waiting for the analysis report on the items we sent in. When I get that I might be able to pick up the trail. But with or without any new leads, I think it's going to be a case where we have to use all our intelligence resources to come up with a potential target and work backward. Now that they have destroyed the laboratory and are carrying around nerve gas, I think it's a safe bet that the time they plan to use it is not too far in the distance."

The DAT-A had just settled around the table for the beginning of their case status meeting when Cheryl came in with a package. She said, "Jack, sorry to interrupt, but I thought you might want this for your meeting."

"Thanks, good call, "he turned to the others, "it's the lab reports. I hope we get something that can put us back on the trail." Jack opened the package.

"It's too early for DNA evidence, isn't?" Rachel didn't wait for an answer. "I emptied the waste basket and took a towel out of the bathroom."

"It is," Jack answered, "but they give us top priority, so maybe it won't take that long. I don't think it will be that important. We know Dr. Ketchum is our main man, although it would give us his background and true identity."

"It sure would be a big help if we found out something about his methods and contacts." Nicole said.

"Very true, but for the moment a look at these lab reports might help us come up with a plot." Jack past out the reports.

"Amazing, I didn't think the Terrorists at the Sportsman's Club would be using makeup. They must have had some female visitors." Todd said.

Jack addressed Todd, "What do you have?"

This report shows evidence of makeup and grease paint on articles taken from the bathroom."

"Grease paint?" Jack asked.

Todd handed him the report.

Jack looked at the report and then said to the team. "Let's kick around the possibilities for using grease paint, assuming it was used by a terrorist."

"Let's add this to the discussion." Nicole handed Jack a photo. "It looks like a strangely styled shoe. It's partially burned and was found by forensic after the fire."

Jack looked at the photo and passed it to the others. "Good idea."

Todd started the discussion. "I've used grease paint when I costume up for some of the science fiction conventions I go to, but the theater is what I think most people would associate with it. In this case though, I think a terrorist would use it in a disguise."

"Maybe it was used to cover up some deformity, like a burn. I'm sure a high risk of getting burned is not unusual for a terrorist." Nicole contributed.

"You could apply the same logic," Rachel said, "to the shoe. Maybe it was used because of some deformity."

Jack stood up and went to the white board on the wall and made notes. He wrote grease paint and under it theater, science fiction conventions, disguise. Next, he wrote shoe and under it deformity with a question mark.

"It seems odd that a shoe needed for a deformity would be left behind," Todd said.

"It does, but what are the possibilities. The person had an extra pair or it was used for a disguise. When we were paint balled five men were there. Did any one notice any one with a deformity?"

They all reply in the negative. Rachel said, "I got a look at one up close and he wasn't wearing any strange shoes and he sure won't be needing them anymore. I can't answer for the other four."

"We're going to leave this for now, but keep it in mind— it may become more meaningful later." Jack wrote target and terrorist's new location on the board. "To locate the terrorists and their target we are going to make two assumptions, unless we come up with different information, one is that D.C. has the potential for the most important and largest number of casualties and two the terrorists have lived and operated in the area.

"Nicole and Rachel, you will use a print out of all rentals and sales in the area. Todd will provide this. Start by checking out areas they have used in the past and talk to all the agencies about any information they can provide on terrorist suspects under surveillance. Interview any informants they can provide. Talk to the three park bomb carries. They may give some leads on sympathizers. We will ask Interpol to provide any photos they have of terrorists who may have worked with the terrorists we have identified here. Todd and I will work on the target. Any questions?"

"How would they be carrying the nerve gas and is there a time limit on its use?" Rachel asked.

"My guess is that it's in some kind of canisters and it would be safe for the time frame they have in mind. As I've said, I think they have the amount they need and have done their development and testing on a delivery system. That's why they reacted so quickly to our threat and moved

out of the KCTC. Any more questions? OK, let's tag
them this time."

Chapter 54

A Bit of Trivia

Three days of leg work by Nicole and Rachel and computer gazing by Jack and Todd were fruitless but not discouraging to Jack—the eternal optimist—who thought that sometimes any small piece of information could lead to a chain reaction which would lead to the solution. His attention went from the computer screen, which Todd kept moving through the various search engines, some classified some not, and at Jack's request, hitting the print key. The lists of targets were broken down into categories; the first list, which Jack considered static, included monuments, airport, subway and White House. The second list was of special events, conventions, and sports events. Jack was looking for a target that would have the possibility of the greatest number of casualties and especially any event where high level government officials would be in attendance. The latter list was sorted by earliest date first and went out a month in advance.

Todd's interest was drawn to one called WCA Convention at the Armory Convention Center on August 10th. He said, "Hey, there's one I'd like to go to."

Jack looked up from a print out. "What's that?"

"The WCA Convention." Todd looked at Jack as though everyone in the world new what that stood for.

"OK, what's that?"

"Oh, that's the World Clown Convention: It's at the Armory Convention Center."

"I'll bet," Jack said, "you don't know that even though the Armory Convention Center is on Armory Street, which is named after the old Armory, the Armory Convention Center is named after James Armory who was a civil war hero."

"What an amazing piece of trivia. That would be a good game show question."

"But we're not working on game show questions," Jack said, "we're on a more serious mission. How many people will it hold?"

"I'll check it out."

"Since you're so impressed with that trivia information, I'll add to it. Don't you think Amory is an unusual last name?"

"Yeah, it's cool man."

"It came about when James' father, John R. Murray, immigrated to this country from Ireland and some immigration official, because of John's accent, interpreted it as John Armory."

"I can believe that. You know that happened to a lot of people when they came into this country. Three thousand."

"People coming into the country?" Jack was taken back.

"No, seating capacity at the Armory Convention Center."

"It has a large target, but so do a lot of other gatherings. No, that alone doesn't make it an important target for a terrorist." Jack looked at the printout again. "The Kennedy Center is having an event and there are a lot of VIPs that are going to be there, but with the security covering that place, I don't think that's the target."

Todd's interest was still on the WCA Convention. "The WCA convention is only open to the public the last day. The other two days are for members only."

"Unless there's going to be a high level official there, I don't see that as a target." Jack was trying to pull Todd's interest away from the WCA.

"How about the Auto Show? It's coming in two weeks." Todd suggested.

"Again, there are going to be large crowds and some important people will be attending, but you never know when they will be there. Let's take a break."

After lunch, Nicole and Rachel joined Jack and Todd and compared notes. Nicole said, "We checked out all the rentals and sales without any luck. We did come up with something interesting in our interviews. When we asked about Dr. Ketchum we got no response. During the first interview, Rachel pointed out to me that there was a reference to someone called Sheik in the cell records of some of the terrorists. When I asked the first interviewed terrorist if he knew who that was, his eyes expressed fear and he stopped answering questions. I asked subsequent terrorist the same question, although at the end of the interviews so not to prematurely end the interviews, and got the same response."

"I think we can confidently associate Dr. Ketchum as being the Sheik and in control of more than one cell. What you have come up with and Matteem's connection with him strengthens that fact. It also tells us that for a man at his rank in the organization, and with the possession of nerve gas, they are planning a major catastrophic event and we're no closer to finding out where or when then when we started." Jack ended with a tone of frustration. "Let's get back to work and review all the information we've got and don't hold back any idea that comes to mind. Even if you think it's silly. It may trigger someone else's thoughts."

Nicole followed Jack back to his office. She stood in front of his desk and waited for him to seat down. An unusual look of anxiety appeared on her face. It amused Jack because he had never seen this and associated the look and her manor with that of a student standing in front of the principal. It also gave him some anxiety because he couldn't imagine what was on her mind.

"Jack, would you like to escort me to a birthday party?" When she saw his eyes widen, his head pull back and his eyebrows drop, she knew this needed some explanation. "It's my cousin's little girl, she going to be ten. It's Saturday. It'll stop those chic questions about anyone new in my life. I know it'll surprise my mother, and you are a new relationship in my life. Oh, I'll introduce you as my new boss. They don't have to know about the other side of the relationship."

Seeing this side of Nicole pleased Jack to no end. "I'd love to go. I can't remember the last time I went to a kid's birthday party."

"Saturday it is. I'll pick you up at ten." Nicole's face no longer expressed anxiety.

Chapter 55

The Birthday Party

Early morning showers cleaned the air and the sun broke out in time for the party —which was good because the party was outside. Nicole and Jack were greeted by Jan at the front door of a two storied brick home and followed her through the house to the backyard where the party goers were already active. The minute the back door was open the noise reminded Jack of a school playground. It was an attractive yard, large by today's standard because it was in an older suburban neighborhood, surrounded by large shade trees which the sun was able to penetrate and leave patches of sunlight on the well-groomed lawn and strategically placed flower beds.

Jan led them over to one of the many tables set up for the party. Jack said, "Great job on the decorating. It's very festive."

"Thank you," Jan replied.

There were many games set up for the children. Nicole spotted one and asked. "Is that a Piñata over there?"

"It is and the children love to break it. Nicole, your mother is already here."

Before they reached the table, a tall, slim woman got up and approached them. She said, "Hi Nicky."

She was a beautiful woman and Jack thought she look like a nineteenth century woman dressed for a lawn party— hat and all. Not that she looked old, she certainly didn't, but what unnerved him the most was the striking resemblance to Nicole. Nicky, hmm, he'd ask about that later.

"Hi Mom, this is Jack my new boss. Jack this is my Mother, Madeline"

"Ok guys, I'll let you talk. I have to make the rounds." Jan said.

"Thanks Jan, talk to you later," Nicole said.

"Let's set down," Madeline said, "I was holding these seats for you. It's a good shady table. So Jack, how long have you been with the American Association of Cacti Growers?"

"A couple of years." Jack lied.

"Where did you work before that?"

"The State Department."

"That's quite a change."

"It is, but a lot less stressful." Jack lied again.

"Now, Nicky, she's more the adventuress type but she seems to be enjoying it."

Jack was uncomfortable with the way this was going. She was either a very perceptive lady or the normal inquisitive mother. Jack leaned to the perceptive lady. "I understand your husband work for the government."

"Yes he was a career diplomat. We lived in different parts of the world. It was an exciting time."

Jan came back holding a tray of food. "Can I interest you guys in something to eat?"

"That'll be great, thanks Jan." Nicole said. They selected food from the tray.

Jack announced, "I'll get the drinks, what'll you have?"

As soon as he was beyond hearing distance, Madeline said, "What a good looking man and so nice."

"Mom, he just my boss."

"Yes, but it is curious, I never met one of your bosses. There is an age difference, but that's not that unusual."

"Mom, you're impossible."

"Yes, and I think the rest of the family will believe he's just your boss." Madeline gave her daughter that sweet smile that says I know your secret.

After they finished eating and socializing with different relatives who stopped by the table, Jack left for the restroom. On his way back he spotted someone who worked in the Diplomatic Corps that he had done research work for when he work at the State Department. He approached his table and said, "Making sure all the kids get along, Glen?"

A surprised Glen looked up and smiled. "Jack, what happened to you? Sit down. I couldn't find out where you went. They just told me you signed on with some Growers Association. Growers Association? A talented guy like you."

"Well, it's been a beneficial change and that's all I'm going to say about that."

"Ok, Forrest, it's just another chocolate in the box to you, but what brings you here?"

"I came with Nicole Burns; she's a relative of the birthday girl."

"That's my connection too. I'm a friend of the family. I knew Madeline's husband when he was a diplomat. He was a great guy."

"Daddy, Daddy, look what I won." She held up a fuzzy looking stuffed dog carried in a cloth bag.

"Good for you, are you having fun? Sarah, this is Jack Dunn a friend of mine."

"Nice to meet you. I have a collection of these and I don't have this one. Wasn't I lucky?"

A sudden high pitched explosion burst out of the children when a clown appeared out of no where and started performing for the guests. One of his gags was to hit the children with an exaggerated, but soft, baseball bat which made a loud bang and the sound of breaking glass. Another gag was that when he proffered his finger to the children and they pulled it, the top of his top hat would open and smoke would come out with the sound of a train whistle. Sarah followed him around with much delight until he disappeared into the house.

Sarah returned to the table and exclaimed, "Wasn't he great?"

"He was very entertaining," Glen said.

I think he was better than a birthday party act. He should be in a circus," Jack said.

"I love clowns; maybe he will be at the clown convention." A look of wonderment, that only a child can have, crossed her face.

"The clown convention," Jack said, "I just read something about that. It's open to the public for one day. Is that the day you're going?"

"No," Glen said, "It's the day after. It's a special show. The winners of the clown competitions and other acts will be put on for the Diplomatic Corps and their families."

In the car Nicole said to Jack, "You seem so pensive, did you enjoy the party?"

"Oh, I had a great time, but I think I could have been wrong about something." He flipped open his V5. "Todd, meet us back at the dorm." The next call was to Rachel.

Chapter 56

A Show to Die For

Back at the dorm Nicole said, "I think we're going to need some coffee." While she was doing that, Jack went to his office and gathered up the case files.

Nicole heard the chute and then Todd. "Hi Nicole what's up?"

Before she could answer Jack answered. "New information. We're going to review it in you're room. We're waiting for Rachel, grab a cup of coffee." Just as he finished this statement, Rachel came in and he suggested the same thing.

Settled around Todd's computer the team watched him start up the computer. Jack said, "I call this meeting because I got information at the birthday party, from a ten year old, that she was going to a special performance of the World Clown Association's Convention put on for the Diplomatic Corps and their families. When we learned of this convention I didn't think it was a likely target, but with this new information I want to get a list of the people who are going to be in attendance. Todd, let's use the Secret Service first. If it's any high level officials, they will have an itinerary. Send it as a priority with a critical classification and give them our identification codes."

Addressing Nicole and Rachel, Jack said, "To bring you up to date, when Todd and I were looking for possible targets, we found out that the World Clown Association was holding their convention on Aug. 10th at the Armory

Theater. It's only open to the public on the last day. Competitions are held and the winners get to perform with other selected acts on the last day when it's opened to the public and most likely at the special performance."

"How big is that theater?" Rachel asked.

Jack answered, "Three thousand."

Then in a somber tone Rachel said, "Probably half of them will be children. It's so hard to comprehend such madness."

Jack immediately thought of ten year old Sarah. He said, "You only have to look at the name of the group we're dealing with, Infidel Bloodbath. Infidels come in all ages."

A cold chill fell over the team and they sat quietly watching Todd enter the world of satellite cyberspace. Fifteen minutes later a, for your eyes only, with a printing block code, a message came back and requested two more security questions which Jack answered. A list appeared on the screen and the group had no need to look at anything but the top of the list.

"Bingo, I think we've found the target. The secretary of Defense and the Secretary of the Treasury and their families are going to be in attendance," Jack said.

"Clowns, grease paint, terrorists, those could be a link to Dr. Ketchum's cell." Nicole was excited.

"And those funny burned shoes that were found at the club could be clown shoes." Todd added.

The solemn mood that had befallen the team when the special performance was consider a target of the terrorist changed when the other evidence added to the possibility of it being such. I t changed to excitement and hope that they could stop it.

"If it is their target, and I don't believe in circumstance, especially when you have items used by clowns and terrorists in the same building, and I think it is, so let's explore the different ways it will be done. I going to start off by saying that the possibility of the veteran performers is small and being infiltrated would be difficult in such a tight community. The greater possibility is the competitors, but this begs the question of how they would be assured they would win and go on to perform at the special performance." Jack looked at Rachel and could almost see the wheels turning, "What have you got, Rachel?"

She said, "It's just that it all seems to be coming together. I thought that they were using the Sportsman's Club as a military training facility, and they probably were, and they were also using it to rehearse a clown act for the competition."

Nicole spoke up, "We came on the scene and eliminated that facility which they were probably not ready to vacate. To be serious competitors, they would have to rehearse right up to the day of the show. That helps us in our search because they will need a large building to rehearse in—and right away. Now we can look for a large building in the D. C. area that was rented recently."

Jack leaned back in his chair and folded his hands behind his head. "Very good, I think you and Rachel should start a new search immediately. A background check will have to be done on all the performers and we will have to be in attendance for the public showing when the winners of the competitions perform. Someone undercover at the convention will be helpful and I going to check that out."

An enthusiastic Rachel blurted out, "Frank, Frank."

A startled Jack replied, "Frank?"

"Yes, Frank. He worked in a circus as a young boy. That's where he picked up his interest in knife throwing. He'd be perfect."

“That would be great. I’ll talk to him about it.” Frank would be perfect as an extra pair of eyes, Jack thought, especially if he is as effective as he was the last time he was just an extra pair of eyes.

Chapter 57

Rocket Man

The Majestic Theater was in Lock Ville. It was along a canal and the old brick warehouses and businesses were rejuvenated with arts and crafts shops, sidewalk cafes, antique stores, and street entertainers. The theater itself underwent restoration with help from the historical site fund and now with the increased popularity of the area it was making a profit. It was rented out for all kinds of events and theatrical productions, so it wasn't unusual for it to be rented now except for the fact that it was a week in August and the man renting it said he didn't want any of the staff that you usually need to put on an event, such as: ticket sales, electricians, stage hands and lighting people. When the owner asked what kind of an event he was doing, he said, in a curt manner, that it was for a rehearsal and that the show was going to be staged elsewhere. It was a new production they were creating and that secrecy was an issue for them. It seemed strange to the owner but the man didn't bat an eye at the expense, paid him in cash, accepted the keys and left. One thing the man didn't tell the owner is that they would be living in the theater for the week.

Dr. Ketchum decided to stay with the group to keep a close watch on the operation. He now sat with Sanjay, in the third row of the theater, watching the terrorists on the stage run through their act. Dr. Ketchum said, "Did you get to the judges?"

"Yes, one a Romanian and the other Italian, but the skit must be really good so it doesn't look unusual for them to win. That's why it so important to rehearse every day. They have to be perfect." Sanjay said in a tone that expressed that anything less was not acceptable.

"And the owners don't know we'll be living here?" Dr. Ketchum asked.

"No," Sanjay replied, "and there are no other employees involved."

"It's very convenient. All the dressing rooms are in good order and even the small kitchen suits our purpose. It makes a good safe house." Dr. Ketchum had picked the larger dressing room for his own quarters—the one with a star on it. He gave a small nod of approval to Sanjay who in return gave him a rare toothy smile.

On the stage, two clowns appeared wearing patched space suits, space helmets, and with rockets strapped to their backs. They looked like something out of an old fifties spaceman movie

"Aaah, very clever, you worked their need for nerve gas protection right into the skit, very well, but the helmets don't look like they will afford much protection." When the clowns got closer, Dr. Ketchum asked, "Are they made for that protection?"

"Not exactly, but they should be able to move out of the area in time." This time Sanjay's voice lacked confidence.

Dr. Ketchum was not involved in the mechanical design of the delivery system, so he asked. "The security will be very tight, are you sure the canisters will get through inspection?"

Because he was involved, slightly, Sanjay took on a hubristic attitude, "It's very ingenious, and there are actually two separate containers inside, one for the harmless smoke and the other for the nerve gas. There is a wire that runs from the bottom of the canister and goes up through his jacket , down through the sleeve and is attached to a trigger, when this is squeeze the harmless smoke is released. Inside connected to the two containers is a shuttle valve that controls the flow from either container. This can only be switched by being activated by a special cell phone number. This will be done just before they begin their chase through the audience at the special performance."

Dr. Ketchum wanted to be reassured. "There is no way a security guard can detect this visibly?"

"No, if they squeeze the trigger they will get harmless smoke. Visibly there is only one valve protruding from the bottom of the tank. Another precaution is that the tank that will hold the nerve gas won't be felled until the night before the special performance."

Dr. Ketchum turned his attention to the two clowns on stage and said, "Begin."

The skit was very professionally performed. The plot involved two rocket men who entered a contest to see who could leap over a canyon. The idea was to leap using their rockets from one ramp to the another. If they both were successful the ramps were moved further apart. It required gymnastic ability, which both men executed well, but when one clown felt he was going to lose the contest he moved the landing ramp further away while the other clown was in mid air. After crash landing the angry clown got up, picked up a stick and began to chase the other clown into the audience. The harmless fog from their rockets (canisters) spread out into the empty theater. The difference on the special performance day would be a greenish cloud of nerve gas covering thousands of unsuspecting spectators.

"Their training has paid off," Dr Ketchum said. "I think they will be accepted as contenders."

"Excuse me; are you in charge of the production?" The question came from a small elderly man wearing a cap. He had a collection of keys, an old fashion, round time clock and a flashlight hanging off his utility belt.

Both men were startled by the question and bounded out of their seats to face the questioner. "Yes, and who are you?" Sanjay said in a gruff tone.

"I'm Hank, the night watchman. I simply want to know if you're going to be using the lighted poster cases. There's an electrical problem and I'll push the electrician to fix it if you are. I called him last week, but I don't think it's on his priority list."

As the two men moved out into the aisle, Dr. Ketchum said in a low tone to Sanjay. 'No people, huh, no outside people involved."

It's was a jab that hit Sanjay hard and by the expression on his face there was no doubt that he could have killed Hank right then and there, but the Dr., the true professional came up with a solution.

"Hank, we won't be using the cases. You see we will be staging it elsewhere. We are not rehearsing it there because we're creating a completely new show and want privacy. These skits are copyrighted and we have reason to believe our competitors would be very interested in seeing the new work before we can get it copyrighted. Hank, I know you are a true professional but I'd feel more secure if our people took over the job for the week."

"Oh, I don't know if the owner would like that and I don't think she would pay me." Hank reached up. Lifted his cap, ran his other hand through his hair and replaced his hat.

"She wouldn't have to know and you would still get your pay." Dr. Ketchum reached into his pocket and withdrew some bills. "It would be an extra week's vacation, which I'm certain you deserve." The Dr.

proffered four hundred dollar bills spread out in the palm of his hand so Hank could see the amount.

Hank's eyes twinkled and he accepted the money. He said, "I don't think the world will come to an end if I have an extra week's vacation, now would it?"

"Good decision, Hank." The Dr. said to Sanjay, "Get someone out here so they can learn the job."

Sanjay called out Acar and when he and Hank left, Dr. Ketchum said coldly, "It's the small missed details that can bring down the whole plan." Then he continued in a more promising tone. "But, the skit went well and it's a solid plan and so close to execution. In a few days we will drive fear into their very souls. Osama will envy us."

Sanjay exclaimed, "*Inshallah*, as God wishes."

Chapter 58

The Pieces Fit

"Monday morning Jack reviewed his notes at his desk in the dorm. He was feeling good about the WCA's special performance being the target, but the consequences of it not being the target weighed on his mind. It would be reassuring to get Bill's opinion and also to get his approval to recruit Frank.

He refilled his coffee, picked up his notes and took the chute down to Bill's office.

"Everything points to it," Bill said. "I think you found the target and I know how you feel, but outside of them telling us the special performance is the target, I say we go for it."

"I'm glad you think that way. Sometimes you get so wrapped up in it and you want to stop them so bad you think you might be forcing the pieces into the puzzle."

"Not in this case." Bill slid the notes back across the table. "You and I don't believe in coincidences, I think the pieces fit."

"Glad to hear it. Now, on another subject, no, same subject another player. We need someone to go undercover and Rachel came up with an excellent choice, Frank. It's a fact, I'm informed by Rachel, that Frank had experience in his youth with the circus." Jack sat back in his chair, raised his open hands and tilted his head down. "I know—Frank is a man for all seasons."

"Unbelievable. I didn't know that. Frank has made quire an impression on your team. He's become a mentor to them."

"He has, and they all consider him part of the team."

"Jack, I'd like to attend that public showing, maybe I can help pick out someone or something"

"You're on. Now I'll see what Frank has to say."

Bill looked over the top of his reading glasses. "You mean there's any question about Frank joining the party?"

Jack thought but didn't say, like someone else I know that enjoys the action.

It always struck Jack with humor to see the sign stating Frank to be the manger of the AACG, it did now when he sat down in front of him. It was like James Bond driving an ice cream truck, although both of them would do it to get a job done.

After bringing him up to date, he said, "So there it is, Frank. Rachel thinks, with your background, you'd be the perfect undercover man."

"I'm in," Frank said, "but that's the easy part. I'll have to come up with a gag."

"I don't think so; the main purpose will be to have you, as a member, mix with the convention crowd on the days that are for members only and check out the performances of the competitors. You've seen many acts performed and you could possibly pick out the terrorists. You know the jargon and how to fit in. I'll ask Bill to arrange it with the WCA management."

"There's a possibility that the team might be exposed to nerve gas in the act of taking down these guys. I'll procure the necessary anecdotes and protective masks for nerve gas." Frank paused and then continued. "If I might suggest it, Cheryl could teach the team how to use the items— she's had experience as a paramedic."

"Good Idea, Frank, you cover all the bases."

"If you agree with that one, how about this, Cheryl could set up the van for any medical emergency and be close by when needed."

"What makes you think she'll want to do this?"

"When she heard about my previous participation, she was a little envious."

"You're a piece of work, Frank, thanks."

Chapter 59

....Three to Get Ready

It was the morning before the convention began and after everyone was settled around the conference table for their pre-op meeting, Jack looked at Todd and said, "You're going to get your wish, we're all going to the public viewing of the WCA's show."

He turned first to Bill, who was sitting on his right and then to Frank and Cheryl, who we're on his left. He said, "Bill, Frank and Cheryl will join us in our effort to spot the terrorists at the public viewing."

He explained everyone's part in the operation and told them that, after the pre-op meeting, Cheryl would hold a training session on the protective gear and anecdotes used for protection against nerve gas.

Looking at Nicole and Rachel, he asked, "Are we any closer to finding their new digs?"

A frustrated Nicole said, "No, but we've checked out many rentals on the list."

Jack recognized Nicole's frustration and said, "It's aggravatingly slow and particularly in this case when you want to see the renters."

"We've come up with a new strategy," Rachel said. "We've been checking out the recent rentals, but what if the place hasn't been reported yet, therefore not listed. I'll let Nicole explain, she came up with an idea."

"An idea straight from last week's Sunday paper that I was looking at over coffee." Now perked up from their new plan, she went on. "I saw an ad for a grange hall to rent for your next event. Then I thought there are a lot of fraternal clubs that rent out their halls for events. Like the American Legion, Elks and Moose clubs, so, because we think they will want to be as close to the target as possible, we are going to use the Armory as the target and check out the possible clubs in one mile increments from the Armory Theater."

"It's only three days to the special performance. Not much time," Jack said.

"After the training session, we're on it."

"Good hunting."

Chapter 60

Is That Frank?

The Regal Hotel was next to the Armory Theater and it was where many of the traveling WCA conventioneers were staying. All the WCA business meetings, yearly elections, and marketing and displaying the latest in clown paraphernalia were in this hotel and all the competitions and shows were put on at the Armory heater. It was the first day of the convention and the lobby was filled and the members were line up at the fold up tables set up and manned for registration.

The man standing at the registration desk was a perfect example of a conventioneer. He wore a wide lapel, red and white stripped jacket, an oversized bow tie and a wide brim, flat topped hat. His pants were covered with patches. His face make-up was simple. He didn't want it to be too close to any other conventioneers whose faces are registered with the WCA.

The man behind the desk, pen positioned over the registration form, asked "Name?"

"Rex Tripp," Frank replied.

The man wrote his name on the registration form and then checked the membership list. He found the name and gave Frank a stick on, name tag and a folder containing all the convention program information. He never mention the fact it was added to the print out and that caused him to spend more time than usual to find it.

Frank walk away from the desk and the first thing he checked was the schedule for the competition at the Armory Theater. The competition started at 9:00 am.

Chapter 61

Bingo

Thursday's activities carried into Friday. So far no specific information had been developed. Todd continued to work with Nicole and Rachel in helping them find locations of interest fanning out from the Armory Theater. He was plotting their progress on his computer. Cheryl was preparing the van with the medical equipment and supplies necessary to treat gas exposure or wounds. It was also used to store their weapons. They couldn't carry any weapons on them during the public performance. They could get clearance, but Jack wanted total anonymity for the operation. Bill called the law enforcement agencies and hazmat crews to open communications with them in case of emergency. This would be kept to a minimum because of the Disaster Aversion Team's goal to prevent disasters with the least amount of publicity. Even though a disaster is prevented, the fear it creates in the public mind is an accomplishment for the terrorists.

If their premise was right, the best scenario would be to get to them before they performed at the special performance. Jack was hoping Frank would come up with a clue to their identity today, so they could all have a chance to verify it at tomorrow's public performance. Jack was the contact between the hotel's and WCA's security. Frank was unknown to them and Jack was a high classified code number.

Jack used his time waiting for a call from Frank by reviewing all the information they had so far and periodically checking with Todd on Nicole's and Rachel's progress, or lack of progress. It was when he returned to his desk that he got the call.

He picked up his V5. "What do you have, Frank?"

"After yesterday's and this morning's competitions, I picked out a couple of acts which could be used to dispense nerve gas, but this afternoon I saw one which, no doubt, would do the job. I waited for the announcements of the winners and bingo. The act won. It's called Rocket Man and the act is carried out into the audience. Later, I got as close as I could to the rocket canisters, but didn't see anything unusual about the design. I followed them to the parking lot behind the theater and saw them leave the area in a white van."

"Do you think they are staying at the hotel?" Jack asked.

"I don't think so. The hotel is right next door and there is easy access to the theater."

"Good job, Frank, I'll notify security to check out those canisters before the public and special performances. If it is them, let's hope we can take them down before the special performance."

Chapter 62

Showtime

Saturday was a perfect summer day and adding to this was the first thing they saw as they approached the Armory Theater. Out of the van widow they saw the colorful procession of the conventioneers in their clown costumes heading from the hotel to the theater. It was like a field of moving flowers. Cheryl stopped at the entrance to parking lot A which was set aside for WCA members and theater staff. The security guard eyed the medical logo on the van and then the Para Medic identification card she showed him. He leaned through the window and check out Jack, Bill and Todd who were wearing scrubs.

The guard moved his head in the direction to the left and said, "There's already an emergency vehicle back there."

"Yes," Cheryl replied, "That's the responsibility of the WCA. They have to do that. We're from the county."

"I see, park down there next to them."

After Cheryl drove away she said, "And maybe not."

When she had parked, Jack, Bill and Todd removed the scrubs, which they had worn over their cloths, walked to the front entrance of the theater and joined the crowd moving into the theater.

Two lines formed at the entrance: one the colorful members coming from the hotel and member parking lot

and one from the public parking lot. When the groups met
at the entrance it created great excitement in the children.
The children's excitement reached an even higher level by
some of the clowns doing small gags. As Jack, Bill and
Todd moved down the aisle, Jack's V5 vibrated.

"Yes."

It was Frank. "I'm right behind you."

The seating was laid out giving members the front
sections and the public seating was behind that. The team
was to split up and try to get aisle seats for a better view of
the Rocket Man act. They didn't have any problem doing
this and when Jack found his aisle seat, he turned into it
and turned back toward the aisle and watched as the others
found their seats. As he did this, Frank walked by and
gave him a silly little grin. Jack just smiled and shook his
head with amusement and admiration. Jack made eye
contact with the others and sat down.

Jack looked toward the stage. Tomorrow the
Secretary of Defense, the Secretary of the Treasury, their
families, and all the other families, without the members in
attendance, would be sitting closer to the stage. He didn't
want to think about it. He didn't have to. The show began.

The theater lights dimmed, colorful spot lights
crisscrossed the stage. The cacophony from the audience
and stage props reached its peak with the silly antics of
clowns running around the stage. And, in the true tradition
of the circus, the Ringmaster appeared and announced the
beginning of the show.

The Rocket Man act was at the end of the show.
When they concluded the act by going out into the
audience and running up and down the aisles, harmless
theatrical fog spaying from their canisters, they were
unaware of Jack, Bill and Todd in the aisle seats taking
photos with their V5. It wasn't a question of who as it was

a question of how. Maybe by analyzing the photos later they would get a clue.

Jack quickly realized that the Rocket Men had to be followed. The V5s were on walkie talkie mode and the team heard the his coded message loud and clear. "How could anybody follow that act?"

Individually the team headed to the parking lot. They all choose the fire exit at the front of the theater because it was the closest and emptied out into the parking lot. It wasn't as fast as they would have liked because they had to buck the crowd going in the opposite direction back to the front entrance.

They weren't the only ones with that problem, Dr. Ketchum and Sanjay were also heading toward the exit, but it was on the opposite side of the theater and it emptied into the public parking lot, though they had no reason to be in any rush.

The three of them jumped in the van and Jack told Cheryl to start the engine and that they would be tailing the Rocket clowns. "Did you see anybody come out of the back entrance?" Jack asked.

"Yes," Cheryl replied, "two clowns came out and loaded something in the gray van at the very end of the parking lot."

A long line of cars was slowly moving to the exit gate. Jack looked toward the gate and saw Frank parked in his car about three cars away from their van. He spoke into his V5, "Frank it's the Gray van, they just started to move into the line now, we're going to get as close behind them as possible and you try to get behind us."

Cheryl managed to pull into the line two cars behind the gray van, Frank to the annoyance of others in the line, proven by a few horns and gestures, managed to get right behind the teams' van. But that wasn't the only provocative move on the line. Just as the gray van was pulling out into the traffic, a black sedan came from the public parking area, knocked over a cone and pulled behind the gray van and stopped before entering the street. The action was received with the same horns and gestures as Frank's move and when the sedan obviously didn't' move out into the street when it could have, Jack thought the driver was doing it on purpose to annoy the people in line waiting to exit. It was a wrong assumption. Dr. Ketchum and Sanjay knew what they were doing. It was a precautionary move from a very cautious man.

When Cheryl did move out into the traffic, the black sedan took the first right and the gray van was nowhere on sight. Todd broke the silence, "That's not good, did anybody get their license plate of the sedan? That was a perfect pick. I think that was intentional. If anybody did I could check it out on the computer."

Nobody came up with a license plate number. "You might be right. It was too coincidental," Jack said, "but we have no way of knowing."

"What's next?" Bill said, "I'll alert the security people to check those two out tomorrow and give those canisters a double check. Do you think we should have the show canceled?"

"That's the problem. We just don't know. What if it's a different method their going to use to disperse the nerve gas. What if it's not the target?" They all sat quietly contemplating the possibilities. Jack's V5 was still on vibrating mode. It vibrated.

Chapter 63

Mixing With the Locals

Nicole and Rachel were met with appreciative and curious glances as they walked through the lounge and up to the bar of the American Legion. The bartender, drying his hands on a towel, asked, "What can I get you ladies?"

"We'd like some information about renting the hall," Nicole said.

"That would be the manager you'd want to talk to. I'll show you to his office."

They followed the bartender out of the door at the side of the bar, across a corridor and stopped at a door with a pane of frosted glass in the top section. A black painted sign on the glass proclaimed this to be the manager's office.

The bartender knocked and said, "Mike, are you busy?"

"Come in."

"Mike these ladies are interested in renting the Hall." With that he turned and went back to his bar tendering.

"I'm Nicole and this is Rachel."

Mike stood up. He was a big man with short gray hair and a pleasant smile. He said, "Glad to meet you— have a seat." Which, they both did. "Now, how can I help you?"

"We've been rehearsing a play that we're producing for a charity benefit and the place burned down, now we don't have anywhere to rehearse or put on the play. The date's coming up fast and we're under pressure to find a place. Is your hall available?"

"No, we're booked for at least the next three weeks."

Now Rachel asked the question which was the real reason why they were there. "I'm curious what events do people rent the hall for?"

"All kinds, for example weddings, bingo, charity auctions, and this week it's a charity fashion show." Mike swiveled in his chair and pointed to an activities chart on the wall showing all the rentals by date.

It was plain to see that the terrorists were not rehearsing here. Nicole said, "We seem to be hitting a dead end, any suggestions?"

"I can think of one, maybe you've already tried it—the Majestic."

"No, where is it?"

"It's in Lock Ville, when you leave continue south on Canal street and it will take you right into the town. You won't miss it. It's the big theater in the center of the town."

"Lock Ville? Do they make locks there?" Rachel asked as they entered the town—she wasn't familiar with this area.

"No, actually the name comes from the fact that this was one of the areas they put locks on the canal to raise and lower the canal boats. This was a busy place and the reason the town grew here. Men and mules walked along the sides of the canal and pulled the boats through the lock system. The boat people would buy supplies here." Nicole passed the theater and turned into a parking lot next to a hardware store.

"Is it used today?"

"There's been a big increase in traffic in the last ten years with the increase in recreational boating." Nicole stopped in front of the theater.

"Sounds like you've been here." Rachel bent her head to view the marquee.

"I have, they have a neat tourists attraction here. You can take a ride on one of the boats and they tell you the history of the canal and town."

They both moved to the ticket booth and then checked the doors. Nicole said looks like it's closed."

Rachel walked over to a poster case and said, "There's sign here with a number to call for rental enquires."

"Good," Nicole said," we'll give it a try. I don't know about you but I'm getting hungry and look what's across the street. The Boatman Pub, we can call from there."

The Boatman bar had served many a thirsty boatman and then some. It was fortunate that over the years all the improvements and changes had maintained the ambience of the original pub. The large wooden beams, the mahogany bar, and the lanterns hanging on the wall gave it a warm inviting atmosphere.

Waiting for their Shepard pies and beers, Nicole immediately started to get comments from a man sitting at the corner of the bar to her left. When he offered to buy their beers, Nicole tried to put an end to it by saying coldly, "Look, we're not interested, OK."

Wounded by rejection the man made a few unintelligible comments, stood up and moved between Nicole and Rachel. He pushed his way between them and in doing so came in contact with both of them. Rachel, like a drill sergeant, shouted, "Back off."

The man said, "Oh, I get it, a couple of lesbys." He then attempted to grope Nicole's rear end.

Rachel punched him in the stomach. He doubled over and Rachel pulled back her arm and gave him an elbow smash to the head. He went down. Nicole and Rachel stood over him in a fighting stance—feet apart and hands waist high. He didn't oblige them. The pub crowd applauded.

The bar tender, who was attending at the other end of the bar when this was going on, came around to the outside of the bar and roughly grabbed the man. "I apologize for that. He's an obnoxious bastard and I've had to throw him out before."

Nicole sat back down on the stool and said, "I bet that hurt."

"No, my elbow's fine."

"I meant him." Nicole laughed.

After depositing the man into the street, the bartender returned with their Shepard pies. "Sorry about that, that's the last time he'll come in here. Is there anything else I can get you?"

"No," Nicole said, "but maybe you could help us with contacting the owner of the Majestic. We called the number on the sign posted on the building, but didn't get any answer."

"No, I couldn't, but maybe Hank can." The bartender adroitly pulled a draught and slid it to a patron on Rachel's right.

"Hank?" Rachel asked

"Yeah, Hank, he's the night watchman." The bartender busied himself with rinsing out a few glasses.

"Where can we find him?" Nicole was enjoying her Shepard's pie.

"You're best bet would be here. He's been coming in all week. Says he's on vacation. Aaah, truth be spoken, he's just come in and is heading for his favorite spot, the table next to the fire place. Here, let me take you over, I'm sure Hank would enjoy the company. Want me to take the pies?"

"No, I'm fine," Nicole said. "How about you Rachel?"

"No thanks, there's nothing left on mine—I'm a fast eater."

Nicole and Rachel stood and waited for the bartender to walk around the bar and then followed him to Hank's table.

"Hank, these two ladies have some questions about the Majestic, I though you'd be the perfect guy to talk to."

Hank's face beamed. "It would be a pleasure to be assisting two lovely ladies, such as yourselves, and what would your names be?"

"I'm Rachel."

"I'm Nicole."

"Lovely names and I've already heard you've gotten rid of some trash in here."

"OK, ladies, I think you're in good hands." With that the bartender went back to his duties.

"I hear you're on vacation this week," Nicole said.

"A bit of good fortune that was, I can tell you."

Rachel signaled the waitress for a round. "This is truly my lucky week," Hank said. "An unexpected paid vacation, two beautiful ladies and them be buying me drinks."

"Unexpected in what way, Hank?" Rachel asked.

"Oh, I can't be divulging that, it was part of the agreement."

Well, back to our problem, we need to rent a theater in a hurry and can't locate the owner of the Majestic," Nicole said.

"I can set you straight there without breaking my promise. It's rented for the week."

Nicole, seeing that Hank finished his beer, signaled to the waitress for another beer. Just one, she and Rachel were sipping theirs."

"And they didn't need your services, that's unusual. I mean putting on a production you'd think they would need all the staff," Rachel said.

Hank leaned forward and spoke in a low voice to emphasize the secrecy. "It's not like that. They need their privacy. They're not putting on a show at the theater. Their just rehearsing a new production and don't want anybody stealing their ideas. The theater business is very cutthroat." Hank sat back proud of his knowledge of the theater world.

Rachel looked down at hank's waist. "Hank, what is that you've got hanging off your belt? Tools of the trade?" Unhook it and let me show it to Nicole."

Hank complied. "I don't use them all, but I feel better carrying them around rather then leaving them somewhere to get stolen or lost. And that little light comes in handy. Same with the allen wrench set, sometimes I need it to tighten bolts and screws on the boxes."

"You've got it very well organized too—I see the top ring is labeled outside doors." Rachel and Nicole's eyes met and, as with partners who work close together as a team, the words outside doors planted the seed which grew into a plan.

"That must weigh a ton" Nicole said. "How do you carry that around all the time?"

"You get used to it, although I do list to the right." This was followed by a laugh and he looked at the next table at his friends who were taking this all in and would be kidding Hank for a long time after.

"I bet that's got to weigh two pounds." Rachel hefted the chain a couple of times.

"No way, maybe a pound." Nicole took the chain from Rachel and did the same thing.

"Ten bucks says its two pounds. We could have it weighed at the hardware store." Rachel took back the chain.

"You're on," Nicole challenged.

"Excuse me," the interruption came from a man at the next table. "Let's start a pool, with anyone who wants to be in on it putting up two dollars for a guess. The winner would be the person who gets to the closes ounce without going over."

Everyone agreed and the man asked the waitress for a pencil and pad of paper. The man next to him looked skeptical and asked, "And who would be doing the weighing?"

"I will," Rachel answered, and after reading his skeptic face continued. "I'll have the man at the hardware store verify it in writing." When the list of pool participants and their guesses were made, Rachel was off to the hardware store.

Rachel went straight to the back of the store where keys are made and handed the clerk the key she had taken off the ring marked outside doors. The clerk accepted the key and asked, "Just one?"

"Thank you," Rachel said and paid for the key. She walked a distance from the counter and replaced the original key on the chain. She went back to the counter and waited for the clerk to wait on a customer. When he was finished, she held up the chain and said, "Do you have something I could weigh this with? It's to settle an argument at the pub." Accepting this as a perfectly logical explanation, he took the chain to the scale for weighing bulk nails and announced a weight of 14 ounces.

Hank with his friends, who had now pulled their table over to his, enjoyed another round bought by Nicole and Rachel. The next topic of discussion for them was whether it was right for the winner to buy the next round. Nicole and Rachel would not be participating in this discussion. They said their goodbyes, which were received with great disappointment, and returned to the car in the parking lot.

Nicole repositioned the car for a better view of the Majestic. They could see the main entrance on Canal Street and a partial view of the side of the theater. There was an ally on the side of the theater, which separated the theater and a brick building on the corner of Canal and Bridge Street, and it ran back to a parking lot in the rear of the theater.

"I think Jack's going to be very interested in this possibility." Nicole activated her V5.

Chapter 64

Rat's Nest

Jack picked up his vibrating V5 and heard Nicole's voice. "How did you guys do?"

"We all agreed on the act with the best possibility and tried to follow it when they left the Armory, but we were delayed and I don't know if it was accidental, or planned. Either way we lost them." Then in a more hopeful voice, Jack said, "How about you?"

Nicole summarized their activities. "Do you think we should go in?"

"No, if you're right on this, the people we just lost may be heading your way. Stay there and keep it under observation. What's the location?"

When Jack turned to give it to Todd, he already had it on the vans GPS system. He said, "Follow that Cheryl and let's see if it leads us to a rat's nest."

"Todd, Google that up," and then to Nicole, "I'm looking at your location on the screen, if these guys are headed that way, they should be there in half an hour. There's a wooded area between the theater parking lot and a path that runs along the canal. Tell Rachel to spot herself there. I think they will be using the stage entrance and will park the van there."

Jack clipped his V5 to his belt and addressed the team. "Let's look at the screen. We're going to check out the theater. I'll be going in with Nicole and Rachel. Frank will take the spot where Rachel is now and Todd you will be on the opposite side. This will give us good coverage of the stage door and two emergency exits in the alleyways on the sides of the theater. Bill, you can cover the main entrance. Use Nicole 's car for cover." Jack pointed at the screen. "Cheryl, you'll park the van in the area Nicole's in. It would be good if we knew the layout of the theater, Todd, see if you can find a schematic of the theater and print it out."

The team sat in silence and watched their progress on the GPS screen as they headed toward the theater. Bill spoke, "It would be a lot safer if we knew they were the terrorists before we go in."

"We have to assume they are, would you pass us those vests that are back there," Jack said.

Bill did and said, "I know, I'm just feeling uneasy about the other possibility, although slight, that they could be innocent clowns."

Jack's V5 went off. It was an excited Nicole. "Rachel just called. A gray van and a black sedan pulled into the parking lot and the passengers got out and went in the stage door. She recognized the two in the black sedan. One was Dr. Ketchum and the other an employee at the KCTC."

Jack repeated the message to the others and said, "We don't have to wonder any more and we can expect the worst when we go in"

"Do you think Dr. K new we were trying to follow them?" Bill asked.

"No, I think Dr. K's a very cautious man and it was routine to him. It's a good example of habitually using methods to prevent being followed. It worked, but he won't know it because of Nicole and Rachel's good detective work."

Cheryl parked the van at the far end of the parking lot and Frank pulled in beside her. Jack opened the sliding door and stepped out to meet Nicole. "Any more from Rachel?"

"No all is quiet."

"Frank is going to relieve her." When he turned and saw Frank come around the van," he added, "or maybe not. You're a neon sign in that outfit."

"I've added my gear bag to the van." Frank was referring to the team's practice of keeping a change of cloths in the van.

"Yeah, but what about that face?"

"I can help there." The voice came from Cheryl who was standing at the opened door at the back of the van. "A little alcohol from the medical kit will do the job."

Jack reached in the van and took out the schematic prints of the theater. He turned and sat down on the threshold of the sliding door. Nicole sat next to him. "Study this," Jack said, "it will be helpful when we're in there. I don't expect much lighting. We'll wear our headlamps but they will be targets in a fire fight and we won't be able to use them if we want to surprise them. We'll wear our vest and remind Rachel to do the same."

"When are we going in?"

"When it gets dark and there's less activity around." Jack then explained the team's assignments.

Frank walked around to the side of the van. Jack said." That looks better, you vested?"

"I am and you know these nylon titanium vests are much more comfortable than the old iron girdles."

A laugh came from inside the van. "Iron girdles?" Todd exclaimed.

And with that Frank left to relieve Rachel. Jack called after him, "Keep your head down."

Rachel returned and put on her vest and sat studying the schematic that Nicole had given her. The next two to leave were Todd and Bill. Bill took Nicole's car.

Jack scanned the area. The street lights were on and the traffic diminished. A shower began; this would help minimize the pedestrian traffic. He checked with Frank, Todd and Bill, they were in position and had nothing to report out of the ordinary.

Jack contemplated the key, which Rachel had given him, in his hand. Rachel and Nicole were standing next to him. "That was a super piece of work you did."

Accepting this without reply, Nicole asked, "What's the plan?"

"We'll go in the main entrance and move to the rear of the theater. There're three aisles. I'll go done the middle and each of you take an outside aisle. The schematic shows the dressing rooms and other facilities are under the stage and back stage area. Two staircases on each wing of the stage access this section. I believe this is where we will find them. Use your silencers on your hand guns. We're going to use a move and freeze tactic through the back section to take them out one by one without alerting the others. Rachel, use the MP5K only if we get in a fire fight, we don't want to inadvertently hit any containers of the sarin gas. We know there're at least four of them in there, but don't let your guard down until we've done a clean sweep."

The three of them with their protective shirts, pants, gloves, and with masks attached to their belts got back in the van. "Cheryl, take us to the movies."

Exiting from the van, the trio went to the single solid door between the large glass double doors and the box office. Passing through the foyer and the next set of doors that led into the theater, they paused and let their eyes get accustom to the darkness, and then moved through the theater.

When the trio reached the stage, they lined up at the top of the left side staircase leading down to the dressing rooms. Jack was first, Nicole second and Rachel was the rear guard. The movement was staggered so no two people were in the same position at one time.

Dr. Ketchum and Sanjay were sitting at a table in a kitchen next to a dressing room where the two clowns were changing into street clothes. Dr. Ketchum stopped talking on his phone and placed both hands, one of which was holding the phone, on the table and sat back. "Sanjay," he said, "do you realize what an accomplishment this will be? Our brothers are very excited. We must make sure this is carried out even at the sacrifice of our lives." He got up and went to the cabinet and brought back to the table a bottle of brandy. "You don't have to join me, Sanjay, but I think I'm going to drink to the occasion."

Acar checked in at the station outside the office at the balcony level and move to the next station, which was the box in the foyer behind the box office. He punched in and turned to walk away, He stopped and looked at the single solid door next to the box office—it was ajar. He closed the door and immediately called Dr. Ketchum.

Dr. Ketchum bounded out of his chair. In a low voice he said to Sanjay, "Intruders—weapons." He then went to the dressing room door where the two clowns had change and repeated the same message. The four of them scrambled for their weapons

Bill sat in the car at the curb in front of the theater with a clear view of the main entrance and saw the door movement and then Acar rushing off. He called Jack and told him they had been compromised.

Jack heard the movement, stopped and raised his hand to signal Nicole and Rachel to do the same. The V5 vibrated and Jack received the message from Bill. He raised his hand displaying five fingers to the others and pointed to his eye, then toward the dressing room and then made a circular movement with his finger. A signal that the terrorists new they were there and there were five of them, not four, in the building. Jack leaned out from the recess he was using for cover. He came face to face with one of the clown terrorist who stepped out of his dressing room and was moving toward them. Jack's silenced Walther popped before the terrorist could raise his Uzi and he went down.

The second clown terrorist stepped out the same dressing room door and fired a burst from his Uzi. This gave cover to Dr. Ketchum and Sanjay who came out of their dressing room, took a few steps down the hall and turned into the corridor connecting the two dressing areas.

They did this safely, but the second terrorist clown paid the price.

After firing at the first terrorist, Jack pulled back into the recess. Nicole and Rachel fired simultaneously and the second terrorist was hit multiple times and his body was thrown back against the wall. Nicole's gun had a silencer but Rachel's MP5K was deafening in the narrow corridor.

Rachel moved out into the corridor to follow Jack and Nicole who were following the Dr. and Sanjay. She turned to check out the rear and to her surprise saw Acar half way down the stairs wide eyed and Uzi in his hands. Fear spread through her body as she realized she would be too late, but the scene before her played out in slow motion. Acar's body was falling before the burst of the MP5K. She saw Bill standing at the top of the stairs—gun still in the firing position. She pointed to the other set of stairs on the stage and then said, "Their heading to the other side." Bill moved quickly in that direction. Rachel continued after Jack and Nicole.

It would have been suicide for Jack and Nicole to follow Dr. Ketchum and Sanjay any faster. They had to maintain caution in their pursuit and at one point, when

Jack exposed his head for a look; it was met with a burst of fire from Sanjay's Uzi, narrowly missing him. This gave the Dr. and Sanjay an advantage in going up the other stairs and reaching the stage door. A route to safety, if only Bill didn't fire at Sanjay who had reached the top of the stairs and turned to follow the Dr. to the stage door, which led to their car in the parking lot. Both of Bill's shots hit Sanjay. Dr. Ketchum made it to the door and swung it opened.

Frank had moved from the wooded area next to the canal and took up a position behind a dumpster across the alley from the stage door.

Todd had moved in closer and from a position at the corner of the building could watch the stage door and the emergency exit into the alley.

When Dr. Ketchum came out and saw Todd, he made a run for the car and fired wildly. Even though this was a baptism under fire for Todd, he was calm and accurate. Frank never shot wildly in his life—he didn't now.

Dr. Ketchum's body was ripped by the bullets and he never got further then a few steps from the bottom of the stairs. Frank and Todd rushed over and quickly pick up his body and carried him back inside the theater.

While the rest of the team swept the theater to make sure there was nobody else in there and to locate the gas canisters, Bill was on his phone notifying different emergency responding groups to the situation there. When he talked to each person in charge, he gave his code number and a Homeland Security code to identify that the cover story for the press would be that the area was sealed off because of a gas leak. He spoke to the Hazmat people and told them to be prepared for the possibility of sarin gas.

Jack had called the disposal team, which they referred to as the magicians, and they had already arrived. Todd let them in and he commented to no one in particular,

"That's interesting, we called in the magicians to take out the clowns."

One of the magicians commented. "Sounds like you've had a circus here."

"Yes we did," Todd replied. "A three ring one at that."

Chapter 65

No Downer Here

It was Monday, but it wasn't a downer, Jack thought, as he sat at the conference table with all the operations reports in front of him. He addressed the group. "That was the Team A's first operation and a very successful one. I couldn't be more proud of your courage and professionalism. It's the nature of the business that you won't be publicly recognized for your heroic work." Jack held up the morning newspaper. "It says in here, on page eight, that the area around the Majestic Theater in Lock Ville had to be block off for six hours because of a gas leak. No one will ever know that it was the prevention of a horrific gas release in another theater that occurred there."

"Maybe not, but some very important people know what happened." Bill spoke as he came in and sat at the table. "I just got off the phone with Homeland Security; Lew Fredrick himself to be specific, and he's elated. He sends all of you his congratulations and said that you have proven the effectiveness of implementing the Disaster Aversion Team and has given me the go ahead to set up another team in the New England area, section 2, which will be called Team B. He also suggested some time off for the team, Frank, that includes you and Cheryl, to do a little recharging. I'm sure you will all find different ways to recharge, good luck, see you when I get back."

Chapter 66

Recharge

Jack and Nicole choose Ocean City as their recharging station, although it would be hard to tell whether Ocean City was as affective as they were at recharging each other. Their controlled passion, induced by their professional duties, was released as they frolicked in the ocean waves, jogged on the beach, smashed crabs, drank beer and strolled arm in arm along the beach looking for sea shells.

Their ultimate time of ecstasy and bonding came in the evenings, as they lay in bed, the sea breeze flowing through the open window cooling their hot naked bodies.

This was such an evening. "Listen to that," Nicole said. "It's a train. It's such a mournful sound."

"It is. It reminds me of a time in my childhood at a summer cottage, when at night lying in my bed I would hear that sound coming across the marsh."

"It's so haunting," Nicole said. She cuddled up and rested her head on Jack's chest.

"I can't describe the emotion it arouses, but it runs deep," and then after a pause, "perhaps it's the sound of loneliness calling for human companionship and love."

"My God, you are a philosopher." Nicole sat up, threw her arms around Jack and kissed him passionately. When they broke she said, "I don't think we'll ever be lonely again, do you Jack?"

"Someone once told me anything's possible. At least we're not for now. Let's hope it stays that way."

www.ingramcontent.com/pod-product-compliance
Lightning Source LLC
Chambersburg PA
CBHW051050050726
47592CB00002B/460